CW00542966

SHE BLEEDS SLOWLY

AN ARTEMIS BLYTHE MYSTERY THRILLER BOOK 10

GEORGIA WAGNER

CONTENTS

Prologue

She scampered like a doe through the hanging ivy, ducking under the dangling foliage and gasping heavily as she sprinted, barefoot in the dark.

Kayla's breath came in scattered gasps, and she paused briefly, panting, listening in the distance. Her thin, ragged t-shirt clung to her trembling frame, and the scent of the forest mingled with the odor of sweat and blood.

Her lip was still bleeding; her hands were scraped and bruised.

Her bare feet were also lacerated from the sprint through the dark woods.

She could detect the scent of the ocean on the wind, the sound of a nearby river gushing over smooth stones.

And then, she heard them.

Laughter. Playful almost. A faint whistling sound.

"Come here, girl!" a voice called out. "Where do you think you're going? Treat, treat. Come here!"

She shivered, terror spiking through her. She spotted a flashlight behind her, sweeping through the dark.

She remained frozen in place, like a startled rabbit stiffening at the sound of a hunter.

She waited, listening, and then...

Something *thunked* into the tree by her face.

She yelped and stumbled back, staring.

An arrow had buried into the wood, flecking her face with splinters.

She blinked once then cursed, breaking into a sprint again.

"Over here!" someone was shouting. "I nearly got her!"

Tears poured down her face as she continued forward. She wore loose sweatpants, ripped at the hems, but at least they gave her mobility.

Her feet were so bruised and cut, now, that the cold ground had made them numb.

She could barely feel the lancing pain spreading through her legs.

She stumbled over a fallen log but managed to catch herself before she fell. She let out a gasp of pain as the rough bark scraped her palms, but she didn't stop. She couldn't stop.

She could hear their voices behind her, taunting her. "Come on, good girl. We just want to play!"

Kayla gritted her teeth and pushed herself harder. She had to find a way out of the woods, had to get to the road. If she could just make it to the road, she might be able to flag down a passing car.

But the woods seemed to go on forever, and the men chasing her were relentless. She could hear their footsteps pounding the ground, getting closer and closer.

Suddenly, she burst through a thicket of bushes and stumbled onto a dirt road. She looked left and right, trying to decide which way to go.

To her left, the road curved gently and disappeared into the woods. To her right, the road stretched straight and disappeared into the distance.

She knew that going left would be a mistake. The men chasing her would easily catch up to her, and she would be trapped. But going right...

She had no idea where the road led, but it was her only chance.

She took a deep breath and then started running again.

Something *zipped* over her shoulder.

Pain flared down her arm.

Another *twanging* sound behind her, and a second projectile ricocheted off the dirt road.

She yelled desperately, still sprinting forward, hands pumping at her side, rushing headlong into—

Bright lights.

Honking horns.

A flare of headlights as two Jeeps skidded in the dirt, blocking her path.

She froze.

She stood trembling in the dark, on the dirt road, trapped in a forest preserve.

She'd come here to see the beauty of the location—she'd heard about Ecola State Park and its scenic shores for years.

But now she only wished she'd stayed at home.

"P-please!" she cried desperately, her voice trembling along with her fingertips where she raised them and held them out towards the men in the dark. "Please!"

The front doors to the Jeep opened.

More jeering voices. Laughter. She thought she detected the faintest scent of alcohol.

"Good girl! Sit! Sit!" someone was shouting, barking commands at her. "Actually, you know what? Play dead!"

She heard laughter.

Then a sudden chorus of *twangs*. Arrows being released from high-tech compound bows.

She held out her hands in desperation, stumbling back.

But there was nowhere left to run.

Nowhere left to hide.

CHAPTER 1

IN THE HOSPITAL ROOM, reclining on the bed, Artemis stared at where her father faced her, his expression grim. He'd even peeled aside the prosthetic nose, studying his daughter's countenance.

Quietly, he said, "I'm not lying. I know it's true. I found information on every field agent in the municipality. I thought I might have to use it one day."

"You're sure about him? And that's why he..." she trailed off, biting her lip.

Artemis' mind cast back to her kiss with Agent Cameron Forester. The tall, muscle-bound fighter had grown closer to her over time.

Ever since Jamie had left, she'd found herself growing more attracted to the uncouth man.

But now, her fear had returned.

"I... I don't think it's true," she said finally, swallowing and staring at her father.

"It is."

"He had a wife?"

Her father nodded simply, his pale blue eyes flashing. "Adelaide Stevens. They met when he was twenty. She disappeared three years later."

Artemis was shaking her head. "And... and why even tell me?" she demanded.

But her father was already extending a hand, clicking his fingers.

She blinked at them.

"Your phone, please," he said, exasperated.

Artemis hesitated, her fingers trembling. She was bandaged, bruised—her encounter with a hypnotist killer in the vineyards of the Cascades had left her more exhausted than ever.

She hadn't spent time with Helen in a while now.

Hadn't been home.

Her father had come to help her on the case, but even he had been forced to keep his distance, to wear a disguise.

Finally, though, she extended her phone to her father and he began tapping away on it. He didn't have a smartphone, as he was still off-grid, avoiding the FBI. Ever since he'd escaped from prison, he'd been living his life on the run.

Now, as he used her phone, she watched closely.

Loaning her phone to a family member had gotten her in trouble in the past.

After a few seconds, though, her father turned the phone to her.

"That's what Adelaide looked like, Artemis."

She stared at the image, frozen in place. Her breath caught in her throat, and she couldn't look away.

The woman in question was quite pretty, with coal black hair, pale skin, sharp features, and...

Mismatched eyes. One the color of ice, the other of golden fields of wheat.

Heterochromia Iridium—the same eye color that Artemis had.

In fact, the same hair color, and the same pale skin tone. The same pulled-back hair.

The two of them could've been sisters.

Artemis found her blood bruiting through her system rapidly, carried by adrenaline.

She looked exactly like Cameron's wife. Was that why he was attracted to her?

He had always been bonded to her in a strange way that didn't quite match with their experience...

And now she knew why.

"Tell me again," she said quietly. "What happened?"

"She went missing," her father said simply. "And then was found dead."

Artemis grimaced, feeling a pang of grief through her heart. Even confused, even confronted by the shocking truth, she still felt pity on behalf of her friend.

Her voice shook, but she said, "How? Who?"

"No one knows. The crime was never solved," her father said quietly. "But I believe Cameron killed the man."

"What?"

"I think he tracked the man down and killed him."

Her father shrugged. "I found evidence of a murder around the same time Forester visited a small island nation known for non-extradition laws. I believe he hunted down the man who murdered his wife and took vengeance." He looked at his daughter now, his eyes carrying a hint of sincerity. "I thought it best that you know. No more secrets." He held his hand over his heart.

And even now, she was finding it difficult to trust him.

To trust any of them.

People lied.

She was surrounded by liars.

Artemis hung her head, leaning back in the hospital bed, feeling a flare of pain through her arm and leg. She closed her eyes, trying to calm her suddenly racing thoughts.

As she lay there, trying to process the information her father had just given her, Artemis couldn't help but let her mind wander back to her recent encounter with Cameron. She remembered the way he had looked at her, the way his touch had sent shivers down her spine. Now, she couldn't help but wonder if his attraction to her was solely based on her resemblance to his deceased wife.

The thought made her sick to her stomach. Part of her wanted to confront Cameron, to demand answers. But another part of her was afraid of what she might find out.

Artemis was pulled from her thoughts by the sound of her father's voice. "Artemis, there's something else you need to know," he said gravely.

She opened her eyes, looking at him expectantly. He cleared his throat, his eyes flashing. "An old friend of mine..." he trailed off now, picking at his fingernails, "An old friend is in some trouble."

He gave a quick shrug.

She watched him now, attentive and alert all of a sudden.

Her father was not the Ghost Killer. Not how she'd thought, but that didn't mean he had given up his manipulative ways.

She waited, watching as he said, "And I was wondering if you'd be able to help me out."

"With what?" she said simply.

"Once you rest up, of course!" he replied hurriedly.

"What do you need help with?" she repeated.

Her father hesitated then sighed. "I have a friend... Someone I met years ago, but we've been close. They've stayed in contact with me."

Artemis hesitated. "Even while you were in prison?"

"Yes. Even then. I once did them a favor, and I believe they still think they owe me. Not that I would ever frame it in such a way," he quickly added.

"Of course not," she murmured.

Her father continued to pick at his fingers, pacing slowly in the door-way of the hospital room.

His voice was low, casual, as he said, "The man is a very wealthy man. A *very* wealthy man. If I told you what companies he runs, you'd recognize them immediately."

"Why not tell me?"

"Oh, I'm not one to brag about my connections," her father said with an airy wave.

Now, her radar was up. She tried to push thoughts of Forester from her mind and focused on her father.

He was still speaking slowly, still trying to flash a disarming smile as he said, "He's a... no other way to say it... a filthy rich billionaire. *And* he's been helping me with legal recourse."

Artemis blinked. "What?"

"Legal. For all this nonsense about being the Ghost Killer. He's helping me find legal recourse. He thinks the state made errors in chain of custody with evidence. It's all quite hopeful," her father said, smiling delightedly and rocking on his heels. "It's amazing what a little bit of cash can buy."

Artemis frowned, staring at her father. "So what about him?"

"Well... he's in a spot of trouble. His daughter, actually. Kayla. She disappeared two weeks ago." Her father winced, shaking his head. "I'd hoped the local authorities might find her but no luck so far." He gave his daughter a magnanimous smile as if he were offering something valuable in the form of his praise as he said, "But you're quite good at finding missing people, aren't you?"

Artemis leaned back in the bed now, resting her head on the pillow. "You want me to find this billionaire's daughter?"

"Well... I mean once you're healed up, of course. No rush—no rush! Just... she could be in a lot of danger. And this *friend* of mine really has been instrumental in my legal case. We plan to take it to the DA in a few months, but my friend is obviously distracted now."

"Oh, I see. So you want me to find his daughter so he can refocus on what really matters."

Her father just blinked.

She sighed. "Sorry. That was unfair."

Otto just shrugged still picking at his fingernails. "Another thing."

"What's that?"

"He's offering a reward for finding her."

Artemis perked up but frowned. "A reward?"

"Yes. A hundred million dollars to whoever can locate his daughter. He's hired others too, but I told him you're the best. If anyone can find Kayla, it's you."

Artemis' jaw dropped, staring at her old man.

Her father continued, clearly knowing he'd baited the hook. "With that money, with my name clear, we'd be able to get Helen the help she needs, from the best doctors in the world. We could be a family again." He flashed a smile, winking at her.

Artemis shivered faintly, hands tight around the blanket across her legs.

"You're serious?"

"Deadly," he said. "Well? Will you help?"

She let out a faint, shuddering sigh. The money was attractive, but Artemis had never been strapped for cash since her chess-streaming days.

She didn't want the attention, either. The rich and powerful played games of their own—ones she'd preferred to be left out of.

But as she considered it, her mind drifted.

A girl missing for two weeks.

Artemis' sister had been missing for nearly two decades. She knew the pain, the shock, the horror that came from it.

The money would be nice. Helen could get treatment!

Helping her father's case would feel like penance for not believing him.

But helping a missing girl... someone whose family was probably worried sick, billionaire or not... Could she really say no?

Besides, it would take her mind off Forester.

"Yeah," she said at last, nodding. "I need to heal up, but then yeah. I'll help."

Her father flashed a thousand-watt smile. "Perfect," he said. "I knew I could count on you."

And then, with a quick nod in her direction as if availing himself of a business meeting, he turned on his heel and pushed back through the door, out into the dark hallway to sneak out of the hospital from the direction he'd come.

Artemis sat alone in the hospital room now, a frown twisting her features.

Forester had been lying.

A billionaire's daughter was missing.

And her father was up to his old games.

She'd been hoping for a chance to get some rest, but now... it looked like more trouble was on the horizon.

CHAPTER 2

ONLY A WEEK PASSED since Artemis' father had visited her in the hospital, and now, as she approached the car idling at the hospital roundabout, ready to pick her up, she felt her stomach churning.

She massaged briefly at her hand. The stitches had finally come out. And the pain had diminished. Her nerves were still causing her to adjust. Not just because she was en route to a billionaire's mansion, but because of *who* she needed to pick her up in order to access said mansion and the surrounding gated community.

She shook her head, trying to calm herself.

Her arm was in a bandage. She walked with something of a limp, though the pain meds they'd given her were doing wonders on this front. A nice row of stitches up her leg helped ease some of the fears she'd had about moving with it. After a couple of days of physical therapy, she found her movement had returned. The pain meds had made it so the movement wasn't nearly as taxing. But she tried not to focus on any of it, and instead, brushed her dark hair from her eyes with her free hand.

Her mismatched eyes reflected in the tinted window of the waiting sedan, and for a brief moment, she was reminded of Forester's wife. Adelaide.

A name that had been similar to hers as well.

"Hey there, Checkers!" A voice called from the front seat.

She felt her stomach sink and stood on the curb awkwardly.

A tall, lanky figure with muscled arms, wearing a sleeveless t-shirt, hopped out of the driver's side, circled around, and opened the passenger door for her.

"And you say I'm not chivalrous," he prattled, his eyes twinkling with eternal mirth.

Forester was wearing cut-off jeans and a white shirt. His hair was messy, as always, as if he couldn't be bothered to run a comb through it. The tattoos and scars along his arms were out in full display, but he didn't seem to mind.

The tall man was holding the door open and extending a hand as if to help her into the vehicle.

It's not too late. A small voice whispered in her mind. *This is such a bad idea.*

She couldn't help but agree.

Did she really think Forester's badge was the only way to access the gated community?

She nibbled her lip, then slipped into the front seat, avoiding his hand.

He blinked at this but then shrugged, shut the door, and circled back to the driver's side.

The vehicle smelt vaguely of aftershave. Forester didn't smoke, yet the car had a lingering cigarette smell, suggesting it was a loaner or a rental.

Now, Forester was slipping into the seat next to her and glancing at her. "Looking good, Artemis," he said in that ever-cheerful way of his, as if he were in on a joke the world didn't understand.

But after her conversation with her father, she knew that he was in on far more than just a joke.

His secrets went deeper than that.

As deep as murder?

She glanced at him, feeling a shiver tremble down her spine.

He caught her watching as he pulled away from the curb, moving onto the street, and checking the GPS suctioned to his window. "Where was this big-wig yuckity-yuck place again?"

"Near the Ecola State Park," she murmured.

Forester nodded happily. They moved onto the highway, picking up speed. He was reckless in most situations, but when driving, he was far more lax. Not, she believed, out of any safety concern, but because Cameron Forester had always been a man to march to the beat of his own drum.

He had dark eyes beneath his uncombed hair and was now scratching at a lumpy, ex-fighter's ear with his scarred hand.

She noticed he was wearing flip-flops with socks, like a true agent of chaos, and neither of the socks matched the other.

For that matter, neither did the flip-flops.

Still, the handsome man gave her a long look. "You're eyeing me, Checkers. What gives? You good? You look good."

"I'm... I'm fine," she said hesitantly.

"Yeah," he smirked. "You're looking real good."

She winced. "Can we just keep things professional today? I'm not in the mood."

He blinked as if she'd slapped him. "I mean..." he was still rubbing at his fighter's ear. "You sure seemed in the mood the last time we hung out. I remember the kiss pretty damn well."

She shifted uncomfortably, her arm in her cast heavy where it rested over the seatbelt against her chest.

"I just need your badge, Cameron. The only way to get into this billionaire's place is with a badge. I tried calling and scheduling a rental showing, but they required a bank account check. I'm a few zeroes short."

"So you're using me for my clout, that it?"

He was still joking, and for some reason, this irritated her.

Partly, she wanted to ignore the issue. Wanted to talk about something else. But another part of her couldn't bring herself to do it.

She looked at him, and found after a moment, that she wasn't as mad as she'd thought.

It hurt that he hadn't told her, but somehow, strangely, sitting there in his familiar presence, she felt weirdly at ease.

She even found a small smile coaxed from her lips at the way Cameron's head was tossed back, his lips pulled into a sort of arrogant, confident, lupine smile.

Adelaide...

His wife's eyes had been the same as hers.

A wife who had been kidnapped. Killed.

She found, out of nowhere, a lump form in her throat. Her hand reached out, trailing along his arm. "I'm so sorry," she whispered. "For what happened to Adelaide."

He went still at the name as if it were some sort of freezing spell.

He stared through the windshield at the road, and for a moment, she thought he was going to pretend he hadn't heard.

But then, he cleared his throat, his voice husky all of a sudden, "You been talking to your dad?"

"Yes."

"Hmm... I remember. Back at the prison. He knew things. At least, I thought he did. Now I know." He shrugged once, and now he wasn't glancing at her, as if he couldn't bring himself to do it.

She left her hand on his arm. Fear was still cycling through her, but she felt safe in another way. Locked in the car with Cameron, hurtling down a highway five miles below the speed limit, she felt safe.

He'd come to pick her up from the hospital. He'd been the one to visit her more than once, even when she'd requested no guests specifically to avoid him.

He'd been the one to throw himself in front of gunmen, multiple times, on her behalf.

He was reckless and frightening and dangerous. But he was those things on her behalf as much as anyone's.

But the thought of losing his wife... Of what he'd done.

She vaguely wondered if that was how it felt with Helen. She'd been willing to go to the ends of the earth to get her sister back. To risk everything.

Could she really blame Cameron for doing the same?

He wanted his wife back.

But he'd found Artemis.

A pang lanced through her stomach. A pang of sadness and longing and... something she couldn't quite name.

Forester was still tense, his hands gripping the wheel. She noticed he was picking up speed now, moving into the left lane as if he wanted to outrun the question. To outrun Adelaide's name.

"Did you kill the man who took her?" Artemis said simply.

No interest in deflection. No interest in pretense.

A straightforward question.

She quickly said, "I'm not trying to hurt you. I promise. I just—I need to know, Cameron. I need to know who you are."

"I'm Forester. That's about it, I think," he said simply.

She hesitated but sighed slowly. "I know. But—"

"I don't want to talk about it."

"I understand, but—"

"Artemis, I'm serious. I don't want to talk about it. Remember my one rule? Months ago? Remember?"

"Don't psychoanalyze you?"

"Exactly. So let's just drop it, huh?"

"No," she said softly.

He tensed.

She found the fear spiking again, and she realized why it bothered her so much.

Forester was dangerous. His mere presence implied a threat. And, in her subconscious, she'd often wondered if pushed to the brink, he might turn that violence in her direction.

In a way, she almost felt as if she were testing this boundary.

"No," she said a bit louder. "I know it makes you sad. I know it breaks your one rule. But we have to talk about this, Cameron. I know she looked like me."

For a moment, she feared he might explode. She thought he might lash out, might yell.

But instead, his shoulders seemed to slump in on themselves. He almost seemed to deflate, as if he were getting smaller.

In a thin, wavering voice, he muttered, "There's nothing to talk about. She's gone."

"But I'm here. And I look like her. But I'm *not* her, Cameron."

Artemis found the words tugged from her lips. A boldness coming suddenly over her. The GPS chirped as they sped along, *Ten minutes until destination.*

She ignored the voice. Ignored the surroundings, ignored the blur of forests through the trees or the distant, gorgeous state park appearing on the horizon.

Instead, she focused all her attention on the man she'd kissed. On the man she found herself strangely drawn too.

"I know you're not her," he said in a breathless voice as if she'd punched him. "I know that."

"Do you?"

"Yes!" he said, his voice rising a bit now, his temper showing. "I know! Please, let's drop it. Seriously."

Artemis could feel the tension in the car, thick as a fog. She knew she shouldn't push him, but something inside of her was relentless. She had to know.

"Cameron, please, just tell me," she pleaded, her voice cracking slightly. "I won't judge you, I swear, I just need to understand. What happened? Why... why do you like me? Is she the reason?"

He didn't answer but shook his head once.

"And the man who hurt her... what about him?"

He was silent for a long moment, his eyes fixed on the road ahead. The only sounds were the hum of the engine and the rush of wind as they sped down the highway.

Finally, he spoke, his voice low and gravelly. "I did what I had to do," he said simply, his words heavy with meaning. "I did what any man would do to someone who raped and killed his wife."

Artemis felt a cold shiver run down her spine.

For a moment, she was silent, her mind racing with thoughts and emotions too complex to articulate. She knew she shouldn't be surprised, given all she knew of Cameron Forester. But somehow, the reality of it still hit her like a punch in the gut.

"I'm sorry," she said softly, her voice barely above a whisper. "I'm sorry for prying. I just wanted to understand."

Cameron didn't respond, didn't even glance in her direction. The car was filled with an uncomfortable silence, broken only by the occasional beep of the GPS.

Artemis didn't know what to say. She felt guilty for pushing him, but also strangely relieved to finally hear him say it.

And another thing...

He hadn't lashed out at her.

With others, he could be unpredictable, dangerous.

But he'd always been safe with her.

In a weird way, it was almost as if he'd passed a strange test. She hadn't even realized she'd been testing him.

But as she watched him, and as he looked away, she found her heart softening even further.

"Promise me you don't like me just because I look like her."

He cleared his throat, coughed slowly, as if to buy time, then said, "I... I'm going to tell you the truth."

"Please do."

"It started like that. It did. The moment I saw you..." He trailed off and gripped the steering wheel. "I hate talking about this stuff, Checkers."

"I know..." She was rubbing his shoulder now, and the contact of her hand against him seemed to give him some sort of strength.

He wasn't a docile, tender man. She knew she was pushing him well beyond his usual limits, and again, the gesture wasn't lost on her.

Her hand was warm where she touched his arm, and she didn't want to lift her fingers.

He said, "Look... Long story short, and I'm going to keep it short. I mean it." He shot her a quick glance. "But the moment I spotted you, I was stunned. You look hella like her, Artemis. Your name is even close. But you're nothing like her. Not really. You're... kinder than she was. Softer. In a good way. You dull my edges. She sharpened them."

Artemis hesitated. She couldn't tell if she was being insulted or complimented.

Forester looked at her and shrugged. "I like you. *You*. Artemis Blythe. I don't see Adelaide anymore. She's there and always will be. But now I have you... Right?"

Artemis paused, feeling a faint prickle down her spine again.

She gave a quick smile, an even quicker nod.

She didn't speak, though, her mind trying to catch up with her gestures.

Then, softly, she said, "Yeah... Yeah, as long as you're telling the truth."

"Do you think I'm lying?" He looked her dead in the eyes. "You're psychic. Am I lying?"

"No. You're telling the truth." She then muttered, "And there's no such thing as psychics."

She leaned in, giving him a long kiss on the side of the cheek, near his lips.

His eyes fluttered briefly as if he were slowly drifting off into some distant dream, but then the car veered and he jarred back to focus, returning his attention fully to the road.

"Five minutes until destination," the GPS said.

Artemis found her mind returning to the work at hand.

"So," Forester said, clearing his throat and clearly attempting to change the subject. "What's this billionaire community all about? Why are you interested in them?"

"A girl's gone missing," Artemis said simply. "And I..."

She hesitated. She wanted so badly to tell him about Helen. About her father.

He'd been willing to be honest with her. Didn't he deserve the same courtesy?

But she chickened out, and instead just said, "A family friend. He needs our help to find her."

"Good thing I have the week off to help you train for Saturday."

She blinked. "Wait... that's still on?"

"Hell yeah. Field competency exam, baby. Looking forward to it." He smirked. "No biggie either, just... Agent Grant says there's a taskforce looking into all of us. And if you don't pass the exam, if you don't join the agency, they're going to be greenlit to start digging into *everything*."

"Wait, what? A taskforce? That's a big deal, Cameron. Why are you acting like it doesn't matter?"

He shrugged. "Because you'll pass. You'll do great. You'll be under Grant's supervision, per the deal she struck with the bureaucrats, and it'll all go back to normal."

He nodded and then turned up a winding road, following the GPS instructions, moving under a canopy of thick foliage.

And in the distance, up a long, winding path, Artemis spotted the mansions.

She paused, though, staring. Her heart skipped a beat.

"Do you see that?" she murmured.

Forester paused, staring.

And then he hit the gas pedal, racing forward.

Both of them had spotted the frail figure in thin clothing stumbling from the woods.

The young woman's eyes were wide, her mouth opening and closing as if attempting to scream, but no sound would come.

Two arrows stuck out of her chest, blood pooling down the front of her shirt.

She stumbled over tangled roots near the gated community. Reached out, red-streaked fingers gripping metal bars surrounding the cordoned area, and then she tumbled to the ground without a sound.

CHAPTER 3

ARTEMIS' HEART RACED AS Forester pulled the vehicle sharply to the side of the road, alongside the metal fence.

Two security guards inside a cubicle, a hundred paces away were looking over curiously, confused.

Neither of them had spotted the woman.

The doors to the car flung open, and momentarily, Artemis' mind retreated from her conversation with Forester, fixated now on the figure laying motionless on the ground.

Artemis cursed, and the two of them bolted forward, gravel crunching underfoot as they raced along the fence circling the mansions.

The woman lying in the detritus wasn't moving, wasn't breathing.

"Call for paramedics!" Artemis was shouting in the direction of the two security guards inside the cubicle. They were both frowning at her, still clearly confused.

One was radioing someone, but she assumed it was for backup rather than an ambulance.

Forester was already beside the woman, frantically checking her pulse. He carefully turned her over, though the arrows still protruded from her chest.

Artemis felt the bile rising in her throat.

The woman's face was pale, her lips colorless.

"We have to help her," Artemis muttered, crouching down by Forester's side.

His strong hands gripped her wrist, then moved up her arm.

The woman's eyes were closed, and Artemis could see the two arrow shafts sticking from her chest.

"She's still alive," Forester said, his voice trembling slightly.

Artemis crouched down beside him.

He was shaking his head. "Can't remove the arrows. For now, they're all that's stopping the bleeding."

The security guards had now reached them too, and Artemis heard them both shout in surprise.

"Ambulance!" she called once more over her shoulder.

One nodded and raised a phone with shaking fingers.

Through the bars, the looming mansions overlooked the scene below with casual indifference. Giant stone turrets, enormous windows, and immaculate lawns stretched as far as Artemis could see within the gated community.

Now, as Forester tried to stop the bleeding, she lurched to her feet, glancing towards the woods, eyes searching for any sign of the attacker.

There was nothing, no movement, no sound.

Whoever had done this had already gone.

The woman was still unconscious, her breaths labored and shallow.

Artemis reached out and took her hand, squeezing it gently.

"We'll get you help," she whispered, feeling a lump in her throat.

"Shit," one of the security officers was saying.

Just then, though, Artemis heard the wail of a siren.

She turned, stunned to see an ambulance *already* pulling down the long road, as if it had just been waiting out of sight.

She blinked in confusion but then glanced at the mansions beyond and realized that the three comma club that lived within likely had their own hospital and emergency teams within shouting distance.

There were few things money couldn't buy, and one such thing was immediate emergency response.

Artemis and Forester stepped back as the ambulance hastened towards them, lights flashing, sirens off.

The bright red and white vehicle pulled over towards them as the two security guards from the booth flagged it down.

Paramedics hopped out. A man and a woman, both taller than Artemis, both grim-faced. They were trim, muscled, and lean.

Even their emergency response teams looked like the cream of the crop. The ambulance itself was also in perfect condition.

Now the paramedics hastened forward.

"We don't know," one of the guards was replying to a question he hadn't heard. "We just found her."

The paramedics nodded, their attention shifting towards the motionless figure of the young woman. One of them pulled out a medical bag from the back of the ambulance, while the other leaned over the woman, checking her pulse.

The woman was still unconscious, her breaths labored and shallow.

Forester stepped back, and Artemis followed him.

The paramedics were efficient and fast. One of them pulled out a device that scanned the woman's body and gave a detailed readout of her vitals.

The other was already placing a breathing mask over the woman's face and setting up a saline drip.

"We'll take it from here," the first paramedic said.

The security guards stepped back, and Forester and Artemis followed suit.

The paramedics carefully loaded the woman onto the stretcher and into the ambulance, then drove away in a flurry of sirens and lights.

Artemis stayed silent, watching the vehicle depart.

Forester put a hand on her shoulder. "Let's go."

She nodded, and together they walked back to the car.

The sun had almost set, and the sky filled with a pinkish-purple hue.

The two of them were silent for a long moment, both of them lost in thought.

The security guards had returned to their booth, talking quietly.

Artemis glanced back at the looming mansions beyond the gate.

Whoever had done this was still out there, and she felt a chill run down her spine.

"Well," Forester said softly, "We came here for a reason, yeah?"

"Yeah," Artemis muttered. "We need to get inside. Then find my dad's old friend."

"Your dad's friend?" Forester asked, perking up.

She blinked, stared. "Umm... yeah, from back in the day. Family friend really."

Forester watched her, nodding once.

He pulled back up the driveway towards the waiting security guards, his badge already in hand to help clear the way.

CHAPTER 4

ARTEMIS' PULSE WAS STILL racing, and she was still shaken by the scene with the woman outside the fence.

She couldn't shake the image of those two arrows protruding from her chest.

Now, though, she stood inside the most impressive atrium she'd ever entered.

They'd been let inside the mansion by a housekeeper. And as the woman had bustled away, Artemis and Forester had been left in the expansive area, waiting for their host to arrive.

"Wow, nice digs," Forester muttered.

Artemis just stared. She'd been in opulence before, but nothing had come close to this level of luxury.

There was an aquarium on one side of the mansion's atrium at least twice the size of *most* houses, filled with all sorts of exotic fish. The water glimmered under the bright chandelier lights, casting a serene blue glow across the room. Artemis felt a sense of peace wash over her as she watched the fish swim lazily in their aquatic paradise.

As they waited, Artemis couldn't help but notice the intricate details of the room. The marble floors were polished to a high shine, reflecting the light from the crystal chandelier hanging above them. The walls were adorned with expensive art pieces, each one a masterpiece in its own right. The scent of fresh flowers filled the air, adding to the luxurious atmosphere.

Suddenly, the sound of footsteps echoed through the atrium, coming from the twin, curving, koa-wood banisters, and Artemis turned to see their host approaching, descending the stairs. He was tall and well-dressed, with piercing blue eyes and a charming smile. He looked to be her father's age, but his skin was smoother, and he'd clearly had some work done.

"Welcome to my home," the man said, his voice smooth as silk. "I'm glad you could make it."

He was all charm. There was no sadness in his eyes. No visible grief.

Was it because his face no longer had full range of motion from all the plastic surgery?

Or was it because he was so used to presenting a veneer that he could mask his emotions.

Artemis did notice the family portrait on the wall behind the tall, graceful man.

Three figures.

The man himself, Julius Bateman, and his daughter and wife.

The wife looked twenty years younger and was wearing a low-cut, red dress that emphasized her own brand of plastic surgery.

The daughter was wearing braces in the photo, smiling. Perhaps sixteen, maybe seventeen. The photo looked as if it might have been taken a few years before.

"Mr. Bateman," Artemis said, nodding politely, and shifting nervously. She'd never spoken to a billionaire before.

But he was just a man. All of this luxury was a veneer, just like his whitened teeth.

She tried to force herself to focus.

"Come in," Julius said, waving a hand. "You'll be more comfortable seated, I'm sure. It's good to meet you, Artemis. Cameron."

He addressed them both by their first names, though neither of them had introduced themselves. And for a moment, Artemis was reminded of her father's mannerisms.

She frowned, but then Artemis and Cameron followed him into a lavish sitting room, where they settled into plush armchairs facing a crackling fire. Their host poured them each a glass of expensive red wine and sat down opposite them.

"Now, I assume you know why you're here?" he asked, his eyes flickering with interest.

Artemis took a deep breath, feeling her nerves start to fray. The woman who'd stumbled from the forest hadn't matched the daughter in the family photos.

At least there was that. Part of Artemis had dreaded meeting this man for the first time to tell him his only child had been shot with arrows. Hunted like some doe.

She still couldn't shake the bloody image from her mind.

What was going on in this place?

Still, she settled, cleared her throat, and only when Forester nudged her, did she open her mouth and say, "I think you know why I'm here..."

He nodded once. "I do."

He met her gaze, and the two of them shared a knowing look. Neither of them mentioned her father.

This man was helping Otto create a case to free himself. And she couldn't forget the reward her father had mentioned.

Julius' gaze moved from Artemis to Cameron. "I hear you're a federal agent," he said slowly, lowering himself into a plush seat and crossing his legs daintily. He wore soft, silk pants that cascaded down his legs. Artemis spotted emerald rings on his pointer finger, and the golden bands made a clacking sound where they tapped against the abalone armrest.

"Agent Forester," Cameron said with a quick nod. "Nice house. Got any golden toilets?"

Julius gave a lazy smile, like a lion who'd eyed a gazelle.

Artemis was struck by this image. She'd never thought of Forester as anything like prey before, but something about the billionaire across from them caused her stomach to twist.

In the end, though, Julius just glanced at her. "Does he know everything?"

Artemis hesitated, didn't look at Cameron, but then said, "He knows your daughter went missing, and he's here to help me find her."

"I see. So not *everything*."

Forester glanced at her, but she refused to look in his direction. She could feel her anxiety rising, but then felt a surge of relief as Julius shrugged, still tapping his fingers against the armrest, and said, "No matter. But yes, Kayla is missing." For a brief moment, Artemis spotted a flicker of a frown. His hand was tapping even more rapidly against the armrest.

But then, he seemed to compose himself, switched his crossed legs, one over the other, then went as still as a statue.

"She's been gone for a couple weeks, I hear."

"It isn't unusual," he replied quickly. "Not with Kayla. She often goes off with her friends into the mountains. She has some... less than *ideal* companions." His eyes narrowed.

And for the first time, Artemis thought she glimpsed a genuine emotion.

Rage.

"How often does she disappear?" Forester asked.

Julius waved a hand, "Oh... every couple of months. But usually only for a week, and usually her mother knows. Though not always."

"Only her mother?" Artemis asked.

The man frowned. "I'm busy at work. Global conglomerates don't run themselves, it would seem."

Artemis couldn't help but feel skeptical. It seemed strange that a father wouldn't be more concerned about his daughter's whereabouts, especially if she had a habit of disappearing for weeks at a time with questionable friends. But she pushed those thoughts aside, refocusing. Nothing about her surroundings, this place, this lifestyle was familiar. It was like entering another culture, a different country.

"Can you tell us more about her friends?" she asked, hoping to gather any information that could lead them to Kayla.

Julius hesitated, his fingers still tapping against the armrest. "I don't know much about them, to be honest. Kayla has always been... independent. Rebellious, even. She's always been drawn to danger, to things that make her feel alive." His voice trailed off, and Artemis could see a flicker of anger in his eyes again.

Forester leaned forward, his eyes narrowing. "And you don't know where she could have gone this time?"

Julius shook his head. "I'm afraid not. I've been trying to track her down myself but with no luck. That's why I contacted our... mutual friend."

Artemis hesitated, nodding slowly. She bit her lip, still picturing the strange scene that had occurred outside.

She felt a shiver down her spine. "I was told... there have been other disappearances. Issues in the area."

"Yes. Which is why this time her absence is more concerning."

"Tell us about the disappearances," Forester put in.

Artemis glanced at him, hesitant. He'd come along to grant access to the gated community. The residents had a no outsiders policy, not even guests unless pre-arranged a week in advance.

But now, sitting there with him, she felt uncomfortable.

Did she really want to do this with Cameron?

She hadn't been expecting him to engage with the case along with her.

But he was leaning forward, and she could still remember the haunted look in his eyes after the conversation in the car.

Did she believe him? Was he interested in her? Or the idea of her?

She sighed, shaking her head. *Focus,* she commanded her mind.

She returned her attention to Mr. Bateman who had cleared his throat, gathered himself, then said, "Not just disappearances. I heard about the fracas outside. Is it true she's still alive?"

"You heard about that already?" Artemis said.

"Word gets around. Whitney Martin. Her family is new to the area."

"I see. Do you know anything else about her? Are her parents also wealthy?"

"Very. Everyone here is."

"I see. And the other disappearances... some have been found, you said?"

"Only one so far, actually. One found dead, that is. I suppose Whitney this afternoon makes another found alive. So there's still hope for my daughter."

He paused, frowned, then said, "But the one found dead was Marcy Thomas. She's Emery Thomas' daughter." He said the name with a flourish of his voice, as if presenting something to them.

But Artemis was woefully behind on pop culture and billionaire celebrities. She just shrugged apologetically.

The man sighed, shaking his head. "No matter," he said. "Suffice it to say, her family lives here. She's a few years older than Kayla. Twenty-four. Well-liked in the area." He shrugged. "I wish I could say more. Three wounds in her chest."

"What sort of wounds?" Artemis asked.

"That, I'm afraid, you'll have to discuss with the local coroner."

Artemis nodded. Her father had been scant on the details. In fact, some of what he'd said didn't sound accurate anymore. Had he been intentionally misled?

Mistaken?

Her father didn't forget information. His memory was as good as hers.

She pushed these rising doubts away, however, to ask, "And you said there were others missing. Besides your daughter. Others who haven't been found?"

"One other. Now that Whitney is back. But the first girl to go missing was Marcy."

"The one they found dead. How long ago?"

"A month. She was found a week later. The next girl to go missing was Rainbow Hulet."

"Rainbow? That's an interesting name."

"The Hulets are interesting and amusing folk."

"And when did Rainbow go missing?"

"A week after the first disappearance. So... around the same day Marcy was found dead."

Artemis nodded now, trying to piece the picture together in her mind.

Four young women had gone missing, then. Marcy Thomas found dead. Then Rainbow Hulet, still missing. Then Whitney Martin, found shot with arrows outside the gated community. And the fourth, who had potentially just gone off with friends, Julius' daughter Kayla. Still missing.

Artemis paused briefly then said, "Do you have any idea where your daughter could be? Any places she likes to go?"

The man hesitated, his eyes flickering to the side. "There is one place she's always been drawn to. A cabin in the woods, near the base of the mountains. It's secluded, and she's gone there before with her friends."

Artemis felt a surge of hope. This could be a lead. "Do you know how we can find this cabin?"

Julius leaned back in his chair, his eyes closed. "I'll give you the coordinates. But be careful. That area is dangerous, especially at night. And with the recent... incidents, I wouldn't want you to get hurt."

Artemis nodded, grateful for the information. She and Forester stood up, ready to leave.

"Thank you for your time, Mr. Bateman," she said, extending a hand.

He took it, his grip surprisingly firm. "Please find my daughter," he said, his voice still steady, his eyes still devoid of emotion.

"We will do everything in our power," Forester assured him. But Cameron was watching the wealthy man with a curious look.

As they walked out of the mansion, Artemis felt a weight settling on her shoulders. This case was getting more complicated by the minute. And the fact that Cameron had offered to help wasn't making things any easier.

She turned to him, ready to voice her concerns, but he beat her to it.

"I think he did it."

She blinked, pausing on the marble steps. "What? Mr. Bateman?"

"Yeah. Cold-blooded as a shark. I've seen more excitement from cadavers."

"Just because he's not emotional doesn't mean he kidnapped his own daughter."

"Maybe. But he's cold."

Artemis sighed, shaking her head. "We can keep an ear out. And before we head to this cabin, I'd like to check with the coroners."

"Does he have your number to send you the coordinates?"

She paused, realizing he'd likely send the message through her father. But then she said, "Yeah. I'll get it."

Another little lie.

How many of these was she willing to tell Cameron?

If only to get her mind off her tweaked conscience, she said, "I'm thinking we have a long night ahead of us."

Cameron nodded, following her lead back to the car.

"Coroner first. What about the hospital?"

Artemis shook her head. "The paramedic said they'd call when we could visit. I haven't heard anything."

"Fair."

Cameron rubbed at his knuckles, sighing and frowning. "Right then, coroner it is," he said, tone grim. "Let's see what new awful thing one human did to another."

CHAPTER 5

KAYLA SHIVERED IN THE dark, wrapping her hands around her legs. Her voice tremored as she whispered through the bars of the cage.

"Please... please, just let me go. *Please.*"

A figure was standing at the bottom of a set of concrete steps. The figure wore a golden mask, which concealed his features. He also wore a dark suit, neat and perfectly smooth. A maroon tie tucked inside the suit, resting against his white shirt like a trail of blood.

The man didn't look at her.

Hadn't spoken to her.

Not in the three hours since she'd woken up—after they'd knocked her unconscious and dragged her back here.

"Please!" she said, louder. "Please! I have a family! My mom, my dad—they're wealthy! They can pay you! Just let me go."

The man didn't even twitch, almost as if he were practicing to be one of those royal guards outside Buckingham Palace, the sort she'd seen on her favorite reality TV show.

She shifted again, her fingers pressing through the cold metal bars as if reaching for something.

She was cold, bleeding along her feet from her sprint through the woods.

She was in some dark, dingy basement, the concrete unyielding against her trembling form.

Sobs escaped her lips, but she tried to hold them back.

Kayla's heart sank. She had no idea what this man wanted from her, but it was clear that money wasn't the answer. She had to find another way out.

She looked around the room, searching for anything she could use to escape. Her eyes fell on a rusty pipe in the corner.

Without hesitation, she lunged for it, wrapping her fingers around it and pulling with all her might.

The pipe gave way with a loud screech, and she stumbled backward, nearly losing her balance.

The man watched her with cold eyes but didn't move to stop her.

Kayla took a deep breath and charged at the cage, using the pipe to break the lock.

She swung it again and again. Sparks flew.

Her fear, her anger, her terror all arose within her. She slammed the pipe against the lock.

But no matter how hard she struck, there was no give.

The man by the door just continued to watch her dispassionately.

She tried striking the door again, but it was no use.

The pipe fell from her hands, clattering uselessly to the floor.

She let out a shuddering breath, staring at the ground, peering through the bars.

And that's when she heard the voices above her.

Low, echoing voices.

Voices that shook the walls.

"This was all your idea!" someone was saying. "I didn't know you had *her* down here!"

Another voice retorted, "You're not getting cold feet, are you? The games are just beginning." This second voice sounded cocksure, confident as if it had all the answers to all the questions in the world.

She found she instantly disliked the second voice.

The first one was saying, though, "I thought it was just going to be a little bit of fun. I didn't know you were going to drag so many into this."

"You should've finished the hunt last night. You got cold feet."

"I didn't!"

"Then why is she downstairs?"

"Like I said, I know her old man."

"So?"

"So!" the first voice was getting louder, more desperate. "Come on! Have a heart."

A snicker now. A cold, serpentine sound coming through the floor above. Kayla's back pressed to the metal bars, and she wrapped her arms around her legs, holding them tight.

Just then, the door to the basement opened and two new figures emerged. Both were wearing golden masks and black suits, just like the guard.

The first new arrival was a man with a buzzed head visible along the top of his mask, the other was a woman with long, curly hair and a wicked smirk apparent through the gap for her mouth in the rigid gold.

"Well, well, well, what do we have here?" the woman said, sauntering over to the cage. "Looks like our little bird has been trying to escape."

51

Kayla shrank back into the corner, but the woman reached through the bars and grabbed her chin, forcing her to look up.

"Don't worry, sweetie," she said, her breath hot on Kayla's face. "You're going to have so much fun with us."

The guard in the golden mask still hadn't said a word, but he watched with detached interest as the woman continued to taunt Kayla.

"You know, we were going to let you go," she said, her voice dripping with false sympathy. "But now that you've damaged our property, we might have to keep you here a little longer."

Kayla's heart sank. She had thought she had a chance at escape, but now it seemed like there was no hope left.

The woman turned to the man in the golden mask. "What do you think, honey? Should we punish her?"

He finally spoke, his voice deep and commanding. "Yes. She needs to learn her place."

The woman grinned. "I like the way you think. Let's go round up the others. See if they're ready for another hunt." She let out a small chuckle, gave a little wave towards Kayla, rolling her fingers, then turned on her heel.

With that, they both left the basement, leaving Kayla alone in the dark once again. She hugged her knees to her chest, tears streaming down her face.

She didn't know how much more of this she could take. The fear and desperation had built up inside her, and she knew that she needed to find a way out before it was too late.

She closed her eyes, taking a few deep breaths to calm herself down. When she opened them again, she saw something glinting in the corner of the room. It was a small object, but it could be her ticket to freedom.

Kayla crawled towards it, her heart pounding in her chest. As she got closer, she saw that it was a piece of metal, sharp and pointed. She picked it up and examined it closely. It was a screwdriver...

She hesitated, staring at it.

The guard in the mask had disappeared now, leaving her alone with the screwdriver.

She hesitated, frowning.

The metal tool hadn't been here before, had it?

How had she missed it?

Had someone dropped it? The woman? The man? Had they been trying to help her...

Or bait her?

She gripped the screwdriver, her fingers trembling, and horror welled in her chest.

But it was the only hope she had, and for the moment, they'd left her unsupervised.

She went back to the cage and started working on the lock. It was a slow process, but she was determined to break free. Sweat dripped down her forehead as she worked, but she didn't stop until she heard a satisfying click.

The lock fell apart, and Kayla pushed the door open, stepping out of the cage. She looked around the room, spotting a small window high 'up on the wall.

Without hesitation, she grabbed a nearby crate and pushed it towards the wall. She climbed on top of it, reaching up towards the window. It was a tight squeeze, but she managed to push it open and crawl through.

She found herself in a small clearing in a forest. A lake could be seen off to her left. The scent of the water swished on the air. It was dark and quiet, but she didn't care.

She hesitated, glancing over her shoulder at the window...

That had seemed... easy.

Too easy, almost.

But why had they left the screwdriver? Why had the guard abandoned his post?

She felt a strange shiver up her spine.

And then, in the distance, she heard the rumble of engines. Like growling predators.

She heard a voice calling out. "Do it right this time. Or you're next."

And then, laughter.

More revving, but she couldn't place the direction of the sounds.

She didn't want to.

Kayla started running, not knowing where she was going, just wanting to get as far as possible from the creepy house in the middle of the forest.

CHAPTER 6

ARTEMIS AND FORESTER ENTERED the coroner's studio to find a body already on an autopsy table.

Artemis hesitated, standing in the cold area, and wishing desperately they'd been closer to Seattle in order to use Dr. Miracle Bryant's far friendlier and warmer working space.

This place was drab. Gray walls, gray floors. No paintings, no personal effects. Nothing.

Just a coroner standing by a corpse, probing at an open chest cavity with a metal implement.

She stared, shivering, but Forester gave her a little nudge, and she took another step into the room.

She cleared her throat. "Er, Dr. Gutierrez?" she called out. "Hello?"

The woman by the autopsy table didn't glance over. Instead, she held up a single, gloved finger—which was stained red—and called back, "One sec."

Finally, after what felt like an eternity, Dr. Gutierrez finished her examination and turned to face them. "Sorry about that," she said, pulling off her gloves and tossing them into a nearby trash bin. "What can I do for you?"

Artemis cleared her throat again, feeling a bit intimidated by the other woman's brusque manner. "I'm Artemis Blythe. This is Agent Forester. We spoke on the phone."

"Right, right... Okay, and this is case number six-eight-two." She waved a hand towards the body. "I was just going over some details to make sure. Why did you need me to check this again? My report is with the police."

"We know," Forester cut in, "but we wanted to see for ourselves. We have a different case we're working on."

Dr. Gutierrez raised an eyebrow. "I see. And what makes you think this particular corpse is related to your case?"

Artemis hesitated. Again, taken aback by the direct question. She paused, cleared her throat, then said, "We *don't* know for sure, but we're following up on a lead and we thought it was worth checking out."

The coroner nodded. "Fair enough. What do you want to know?"

Forester stepped forward, pulling out a pad of paper and a pen. "Can you tell us anything about the cause of death?"

Dr. Gutierrez sighed. "Well, I can't say for sure until I get the results of the toxicology report, but it looks like this person died from a drug overdose. There were high levels of fentanyl in their system."

Artemis felt a knot form in her stomach. Fentanyl was a powerful opioid.

She paused, "But what about the wounds? I heard she was stabbed three times."

"She was," the coroner responded, "But it was post-mortem."

"Someone stabbed her after she'd died?"

"Exactly."

Artemis glanced at Forester now. Both of them were sharing confused looks. Artemis said, "This is the body of Marcy Thomas, isn't it?"

"That's right." A nod.

"So... so, she overdosed then was stabbed—why would anyone do that?"

"I don't know."

The coroner wasn't volunteering any further information, and Artemis could feel her nerves rising again. She wasn't sure how Forester did this for a living, constantly questioning difficult sorts.

She sighed, though, realizing that eventually, within a week, she'd have to take the field test and gain her own credentials as an agent.

If not, things would sour quickly.

According to Forester, a taskforce had been assigned to investigate them and their *outside-the-box* approach to cases.

The last thing Artemis and her family needed right now was more scrutiny.

She sighed, leaning back and crossing her arms. She approached the table now, glancing towards a gray container resting next to a worn t-shirt.

"Is this her stuff?" Artemis asked.

"Mhmm." The coroner had returned her attention to the cadaver again, leaving Artemis to study Marcy Thomas' personal effects.

As Artemis examined Marcy Thomas' belongings, she couldn't help but feel a sense of sadness. The t-shirt was well-worn and had a faded logo of a band Artemis had never heard of. There was a picture of a small child in a locket that hung from a chain. It was clear that the woman's life had been cut short, and Artemis couldn't help but wonder who would want to do this to her.

She picked up the locket and examined the picture inside. The child had a bright smile and big, innocent eyes. Artemis felt a pang of guilt in her chest. She was supposed to be solving this case, but her mind was distant, distracted.

Not just with fears and doubts... but hopes too.

Was she a bad person for thinking about the hundred-million reward for finding the billionaire's daughter?

Now that she thought about it, though... Julius hadn't *seemed* like the type to offer so much of his personal wealth—not even for his daughter.

In a way, he'd seemed cold and distant.

She wondered if Forester was right. Maybe they needed to take a second look at the man hiring them.

She fingered the locket, studying the child.

It was an older image, and the golden hair and green eyes matched Marcy's own features.

Artemis turned the locket over. *M.T. 5.*

Marcy Thomas. Five.

Why did Marcy wear a picture of herself around her neck? Not just of herself, but of when she'd been a child?

Curious.

Artemis' brow wrinkled as she fingered the locket, then placed it back on the clothing. Her attention then turned towards a plastic bag.

Within the bag, she spotted an arrowhead.

Artemis stared. "Was this found on the body?" she said.

The coroner glanced over, then nodded. "It was used to perforate the corpse after death."

"After she overdosed."

"Or was drugged."

Artemis frowned, staring at the arrowhead. She leaned in, studying it.

The thing wasn't some old-fashioned souvenir found by some river bed. It was the top couple inches of a sleek, carbon-fiber, reinforced shaft with a pinkie-sized, angled, metal head.

The shaft was stained in copper.

But as she stared at it, Forester said, "Looks like Bozeman arrows."

"What's that?" She glanced back.

He waved at the item inside the evidence bag. "I go Elk hunting with Wade some summers. He uses a bow. Bozeman arrows. That's the brand that uses those carbon-fiber shafts stained purple like that.

Artemis glanced back at the evidence bag.

"How common are those?"

He shook his head. "Very rare. Super expensive. Wade's family comes from money."

Artemis held the bag now, studying the arrow. "Is there a way to find out what company sold these in the area?"

Forester nodded. "Yeah, I can make some calls and see if there are any local stores that sell Bozeman arrows."

Artemis handed the bag back to the coroner and turned to Forester. "Good. Let's follow up on that lead. Maybe we can find out who owns these arrows and if they have any connection to Marcy Thomas' death."

Forester nodded in agreement, bid farewell to the coroner, and was turning to leave when the coroner cleared her throat and said, "One other thing."

They both glanced back.

"Marcy died from fentanyl, but there was another drug in her system. Something that didn't register on the tox report."

"What does that mean?" Artemis asked, hands on her hips as she turned back to face the woman.

"It means," the no-nonsense coroner said, matching Artemis' posture, "That there's some new street drug out there. Something so new that we don't even have it logged in our database."

"Might mean she was the one cooking it," Forester pointed out. "Sampling her own supply before taking it to market."

"It's not a bad thought. I've seen that sort of thing before down here."

Artemis nodded, her mind racing with possibilities. She had heard of new street drugs before, but it was rare that they were completely untraceable. If Marcy had been cooking it herself, then there was a chance that she had some sort of connection to the people who were selling it.

"We need to find out more about this drug," Artemis said, turning to Forester. "See if there have been any other cases where it's been found."

"I'll get on it," he said. "But in the meantime, maybe we should start asking around the streets. See if anyone knows anything. I've got my connections on the corners."

Artemis nodded, knowing that it was a long shot, but it was worth a try. She glanced back at the coroner. "Thank you for your help," she said.

The woman nodded and began to pack up her things. Artemis and Forester left the morgue and stepped out into the bright sunlight. Artemis shielded her eyes, feeling a headache coming on.

"What do you think, Art?" Forester asked, studying her. "You seem distracted."

Artemis sighed, running a hand through her hair. "I don't know," she said. "I keep thinking about the callous indifference Julius seemed to have about his daughter. If he is so concerned to offer a cash reward for Kayla then why doesn't it seem like he cares if we find her or not?"

Forester paused, wrinkling his nose. "I mean... I've already told you what I think. But hang on, *what* cash reward?"

"I didn't mention it?"

"No."

"A hundred million," she said simply.

He gaped at her.

She hid a smile.

"You're joking?"

"Not at all. If we find Kayla, the reward is a hundred mil."

Artemis and Forester stood silently for a moment, both trying to wrap their minds around the exorbitant amount of money that was being offered. It was more than either of them had ever seen in their lives, and it was almost too much to comprehend.

After a moment, Forester spoke up. "Do you think that's why Julius is so cold about the whole thing? Maybe he's resentful that it's going to cost him that much."

Artemis shook her head. "I don't know. It just seems strange. I mean, I know that a hundred million is a lot of money, but if he really cared about his daughter, you'd think he'd be more invested in finding her himself."

"Maybe he's just not the hands-on type," Forester suggested. "I mean, he's a billionaire. He's got people to do that sort of thing for him."

Artemis considered that for a moment then nodded. "You're right. It's just... something about the whole thing doesn't sit right with me. We need to keep digging."

Forester nodded in agreement. "Agreed. I'll start making calls about those arrows, and then we can start asking around about that new drug."

Artemis nodded, and the two of them moved back in the direction of their parked car.

The sun was high in the sky, but a cloud was rolling in, bringing darkness with it.

As she walked, she noticed a figure watching them from across the street.

A man, standing on the curb, wearing golden sunglasses and a black suit.

The moment the man realized she'd spotted him, he turned and slipped into the front seat of an SUV with tinted windows.

The car churned up dust and sped away.

CHAPTER 7

SHE HESITATED, STARING AFTER the car driven by the man who'd been watching them outside the coroner's office.

Then she murmured, "Forester..."

"Hmm?" He was already inside, starting the engine.

"Can we follow those guys?"

"What?"

"That car. I think I saw them outside Julius' mansion. And now they've followed us here."

"Really?"

"Yeah. The license plate is different. I think they switched it."

Forester frowned, and Artemis hastened into the front seat. The lead on the street drug and the expensive arrowheads could wait. Maybe the killer had gotten too close.

Maybe the killer had followed them here and thought he was able to get away without being stopped.

"Faster, Cameron!" Artemis said as they pulled up the street, moving in behind the fleeing SUV.

Suddenly, the SUV veered off the side of the road, hopping a curb, and speeding down an alley.

"They made us!" Cameron cried out.

"They're bolting—don't lose him!"

Forester shouted, "Buckle up! Hang on tight."

And then he spun the wheel, taking them up and over the curb in a move that rattled Artemis' teeth.

It looked like the SUV was making a beeline for an underpass beneath a bridge.

Artemis and Forester were hot on their tail as they followed the SUV into the underpass. The darkness swallowed them whole, and the only sounds were the revving of their engine and the screeching of the SUV's tires. Artemis gripped the door handle tightly, her heart racing as they closed in on the SUV. Forester was focused, his eyes fixed on the car in front of them.

The SUV suddenly spun out of control, its back end fishtailing as it came to a stop. Forester hit the brakes hard, and they came to a halt behind the SUV. Artemis and Forester exchanged a look, then got out of the car, drawing their guns.

The driver's door of the SUV opened, and a man stepped out. He was tall and muscular, with a shaved head and a sneer on his face behind his golden glasses. He wore black jeans and a leather jacket, and he had a gun in his hand.

"What the hell!" the man snapped, glaring at both of them. "You trying to get us killed?"

"Drop the weapon!" Forester snapped, pointing his own firearm at the man. "Drop it now!"

"Easy, big guy," said the muscle-bound gunman. He rolled his shoulders, his suit sleeves crinkling. "I'm private security, for Mr. Bateman. Don't shoot—I've got ID in my pocket. Can I reach for it?"

The guy's sneer had faded, and now he spoke with a cocksure, confident tone as if he were completely in control of the situation.

The headlights from the cars cast his shadow in different directions where he stood by the open front door of his vehicle.

Forester's own firearm didn't waver.

Artemis observed the man's body language, noting the way he kept his hand steady on his gun. She knew that this was a delicate situation and that one wrong move could lead to disaster.

"Slowly," she said, speaking with far more confidence than she felt. "And keep your hands where we can see them."

The man nodded, and reached into his pocket, pulling out a wallet, fumbling with it briefly. "Here, just... just point that thing someplace else, okay?" he said, glancing at Forester and frowning.

The man looked like a skinhead in a black suit, showing the occasional tattoo poking up past his collar. He had the faintest pungent odor of clove cigarettes and black coffee emanating from him, which Artemis could smell over the stench of burning rubber.

As he fumbled with his wallet, Artemis and Forester exchanged a glance, then Cameron lowered his weapon.

"What's going on?" Forester asked, his tone suspicious. "Why were you following us?"

The man shrugged, tucking his own gun back into his waistband. "Just doing my job. Mr. Bateman has a lot on the line, as I'm sure you know. He wanted to make sure that you two were up to the job. That you weren't going to cause trouble."

Artemis frowned. "Why would he think we were going to cause trouble?"

The man smirked. "You're investigating the disappearance of his daughter. That tends to make people nervous. Not to mention, he had some other PIs who got paid some upfront then disappeared."

The man shrugged. "Makes a soul suspicious is all."

Artemis and Forester exchanged another look.

"What do you know about Kayla's disappearance?" Artemis asked, her voice steady.

The man's smirk widened. "I don't know anything. But I can tell you this—if you want to keep your nose clean, you'll stay away from Mr. Bateman and his business."

Artemis hesitated. She glanced at his wallet. He hadn't opened it yet. "Can we see that ID?" she asked.

The man's expression flickered.

His eyes darted at her.

He swallowed briefly.

Then he said, "Ah, good. Right on time."

She heard the screech of tires a second later.

She spun around, staring. A jeep was speeding towards them, racing down the open tunnel. Horn blaring, lights flashing.

Two men pushed out of the rear windows, and Artemis spotted the guns in their hands.

Suddenly, the man who had claimed to be security for Bateman—but hadn't shown them any ID—raised a second weapon which he'd had hidden in his left hand.

He fired, aiming at Forester's back.

But Artemis had spotted the movement. She'd shoved Cameron at the last moment.

Something hot grazed her arm. But the two of them hit the ground behind their bumper.

A spray of bullets missed them from the jeep and from the fake security guard's handgun.

Forester spun around from where he lay on the asphalt, releasing a shot of his own.

The skinhead cursed, his leg knocked out from under him where a bullet had caught his shin.

The man gasped in pain, limping desperately back to the open door of his car.

The jeep had spun around again, lights still flashing.

Backup.

The skinhead had been stalling for backup.

He wasn't a security guard.

He was something else.

More bullets skipped off the concrete, though, and Artemis was forced to cower behind the wheel of their own sedan, keeping cover as bullets skipped off the metal hood, sending showers of sparks raining down on her.

Artemis heard Forester call out, his voice strained. "You okay?"

She nodded, her heart pounding in her chest. She could feel the heat radiating from the wheel at her back, but she pushed the discomfort from her mind.

The two men from the jeep remained in their vehicle and were shouting instructions at the limping man.

Whenever Artemis tried to glance out, a new wave of lead hit the car, keeping her down.

"Covering fire," Forester muttered. "Just stay put. They'll pass by soon enough."

"I think that skinhead has something to do with the murders," Artemis whispered. "He has to. He knows about Bateman. About everything!"

Forester paused, eyes narrowing.

Then, he extended his weapon towards her. "I need you to give me cover."

She stared at the gun, her eyes as wide as saucers.

Marksmanship was the one area she constantly failed in when practicing for the field test.

Now, the gun felt heavy in her hand.

"Ready?" Forester said.

"Wait... what are you doing?"

"Set."

"No, Cameron! CAMERON!"

"GO!" he yelled.

And then Agent Forester surged up, sprinting around the back of the car and emerging from cover.

Gunfire erupted a second later.

CHAPTER 8

ARTEMIS ONLY HAD A split second to react as Forester emerged from behind the car.

Instincts took over.

Cameron had been helping her train over the last few weeks, ever since Supervising Agent Grant had told her that the feds weren't going to press charges for the time she'd been on the run.

But they still didn't trust her, and so in exchange for not pressing charges, they'd required that she spend at least two years working directly under Agent Grant in an official position.

That required her to pass the FBI field test.

It required her to shoot straight.

But try as she might, her aim was suspect.

And now, as she emerged behind the car, firing, she missed the gunmen jammed out of the Jeep's window.

The vehicle with the blaring headlights had come to a stop across the street, under the tunnel.

The skinhead with the limp, who Cameron had shot, was now making his getaway, having slipped back into his SUV. He left twin streaks of rubber on the ground as he zipped away from them.

Artemis' first bullet struck the Jeep's tire; the second hit the door.

The tire burst with an explosion, and the Jeep, which had been picking up speed again, veered off course, slamming into the wall.

"Shit," she cursed.

She continued to fire, making sure the two gunmen were ducked low to avoid the bullets.

This gave Cameron time to sprint across the street, covering the distance like a gazelle.

Or more like a Cheetah—with really big fangs.

The ex-fighter lunged through the air as he reached the jeep, throwing himself forward and grabbing the first gunman by the collar.

Artemis stopped firing, staring in awe and some fear as Forester ripped the shooter out of the car *through* the window, snarling as he did.

It didn't look like it cost Cameron anything to do it. He tossed the man over his shoulder, almost lazily, sending him pirouetting through the air. He hit the ground with a *thump,* his gun clattering away.

The second gunman was screaming, trying to shoot Cameron, but Forester had reached through the window and snatched his wrist.

There was a crunching sound then a shout of pain.

Cameron ripped the second man out of the car, or at least tried to, but the seatbelt stopped him.

"Click it!" Forester snarled, pointing. "I said click it, or I'll feed you your eyes!"

The man yelped and clicked his seatbelt. There was a whirring sound, then a scream as Forester pulled the second gunman out of the front seat and flung him on top of the first—the first man had started to rise but was struck, and the two of them went stumbling once more.

Then Forester was on them.

Two against one. It was hardly a fair fight.

Without their guns, the men didn't stand a chance against the trained cage-fighter.

Artemis watched in awe as Forester took down the two men with a series of punches and kicks. He moved with such speed and precision, it was like watching a dance. The two men scrambled to get up, but Forester was relentless, never giving them a chance to catch their breath.

One of the men managed to land a punch on Forester's jaw, but it only seemed to encourage him. He responded with a brutal knee to the man's gut, causing him to double over in pain.

The other man tried to make a run for it, but Forester was too quick. He grabbed the man by the collar and slammed him onto the ground, knocking the wind out of him.

Artemis couldn't help but in equal parts admire and fear Forester's skill. He was like a force of nature, unstoppable and unyielding. She knew that he had a past in cage-fighting, but seeing it in action was something else entirely.

As Forester held the man to the ground, though, the second figure pulled a knife from his sleeve.

She tried to shout a warning as the man lunged forward.

But Cameron was distracted by the assailant on the ground.

So she raised her gun and fired.

Her bullet struck the knife-wielding thug's shoulder, sending him reeling.

He yelped as the knife fell from his hand.

Forester whirled around, spotting the knife, then glancing at Artemis.

"Thanks," he said, sweat pouring down his face.

Her eyes widened. "Get down!"

Cameron didn't hesitate. Didn't look to see where she was watching.

But he threw himself to the ground.

Another burst of bullets spat over him. This time from an automatic weapon.

A third gunman. They hadn't seen him in the car. Perhaps the driver? Someone in the back?

Artemis took two surging steps forward, dragging Cameron back behind the car.

The bullets would've hit them, she supposed, if the shooter inside the vehicle had been an experienced gunman.

But his aim was as bad as hers.

The bullets sprayed across the ground, though.

And the voice from inside the car was screaming, "Get in! Get in now!"

Sirens could be heard in the distance.

Horns were honking from the entrance to the tunnel. Witnesses were arriving on scene.

Artemis breathed heavily, hidden against the wheel as the Jeep was boarded once more.

The three men were cursing as they hit the gas and then sped away, their busted tire leaving sparks where metal rim hit asphalt.

A squeal of tires later, Artemis and Forester were left alone once again, both breathing heavily in the dark, crouched by the car, motionless and quiet.

CHAPTER 9

IT WAS EVENING BY the time they'd filed their report, and Agent Cameron Forester was in a bad mood.

He massaged at his knuckles, which were scraped and bruised, while leaning back in the metal chair facing a sturdy desk.

He and Artemis had been tucked away by the locals in the basement of the municipal precinct.

Artemis' arm, which had still been wrapped in a bandage from her previous escapades, was now being treated to a massage.

The pretty, pale woman with the mismatched eyes sat by a window, rubbing ruefully at her arm, and wincing every now and then.

Whenever she wasn't looking, he shot her a glance, studying her features, her silhouette.

"Are we sure they got away?" Artemis asked, glancing back at him.

Forester nodded, his phone resting on the desk where bulletin updates flashed across the screen. "They're gone."

"Dammit," she murmured.

He just nodded in agreement.

Artemis looked back at her laptop which rested on the table in front of her.

Evening had come quickly, and the final rays of sunshine were fading beyond the horizon, streaking the oak table where Artemis sat and looked through the window.

"I think I may have found something," she said at last.

Forester glanced over.

"Bozeman arrows," Artemis said, turning the screen so he could see. "You were right. Most places don't stock them, and the few that claim to are all out. But this one spot claims it orders them special. Charges a premium." She whistled softly, staring at the screen.

"How much?" he queried.

"A grand per pop," she said.

"Per quiver?"

"Per arrow."

"Shit."

Forester shook his head, dragging a hand over his features.

"Guess we're both in the wrong line of work," Artemis muttered.

He couldn't disagree. He pushed from his chair, stretching as he approached her, wincing occasionally as he felt a lance of pain through his bruised ribs and scraped arm.

But whenever she looked, he pretended as if the pain didn't bother him.

He wasn't sure how he was supposed to act around Artemis Blythe.

Again, as he approached, and as she leaned in reading about the arrows, his mind drifted away.

His wife... Dead seven years ago.

And he'd found the man who'd done it.

He frowned.

She knew now.

Her father must've told her.

And yet... it was as if things were no different between them. As if she were more than willing to let things stay the way they were.

They'd spoken in the car. Or, at least, she had. But Forester found it difficult.

As someone whose mind didn't make the usual emotional connections, it was like having culture shock whenever he was dragged unwillingly back into the realm of grief and loss.

She'd been the only person who'd aroused emotion in him. The only person he'd been psychologically capable of forming a connection with. Sociopaths could sometimes latch onto one or two very special people.

Otherwise, emotional connections were difficult.

He'd thought he'd lost his only source of *true* feeling when his wife had died.

But that had changed when he met Artemis.

Her eyes crinkled very slightly in the corners as she grew excited, her fingers increasing in speed as they clacked across the keyboard.

It was the small things.

The way she drew joy from solving even the simplest of puzzles. Her loyalty to her family. Her love. Her kindness and compassion.

Her beauty, though she didn't wear makeup, didn't accentuate her features, and often wore bulky sweaters.

None of it really mattered.

She was... different than anyone he'd met.

She did look like his wife. He knew it. He'd *known* it. Even her mismatched eyes. But...

But it wasn't a replacement.

Almost like a rebirth. As if life were giving him a second chance with the woman of his dreams.

As this thought flashed through his mind, he felt his cheeks warming, and his hands tensed at his sides. *Woman of his dreams...* what sort of asshole thought like that?

And yet... that flush across his cheeks, the warming in his chest. More evidence that his emotions were returning. His *heart* was feeling.

"What?" He blinked. Artemis was staring at him. "What's wrong?"

He hadn't realized he'd been staring at her. "Oh... Umm..." He scratched at his chin. "My bad. Just, the arrows? Who's the supplier?"

He cleared his throat hesitantly and refused to meet her gaze as he leaned over her, peering at the computer screen.

She paused, but then didn't press the issue and instead tapped a finger against the green and yellow masthead on the site. "Looks like it's called *Tandem Importing.* Their headquarters isn't far from here. They don't sell retail, but maybe people in the area can go direct to the source. With money like these guys have..." She trailed off and shrugged.

Forester nodded. "Got an address?"

"Yeah." Artemis took a screenshot with her phone of the *Contact Us* section.

Then, she pushed to her feet, rubbing at her arm again, and tugging the sweater sleeve lower over the white wrapping around her wrist.

As Artemis turned to the door, she glanced at him again. "So?" she said.

"Umm... sorry, what?"

"The APB? Any news?"

Relieved she was talking about the men who'd shot at them rather than anything as serious as human emotions, he checked his phone. "Nah. Nothing. They're gone."

She frowned, shaking her head. "They must have some sort of help in the area."

"Yeah. Yeah, definitely. The rules are different on this one. Money talks, but it also walks and hides and any other damn verb you can think of. Especially funny money."

Artemis bit her lip. "Those weapons they used... Powerful. I felt like I was in a warzone."

"Same. You did well though."

"You too. So, wanna check out this *Tandem Importing?* If we can find who shot that arrow, we can find the killers."

"Deal. I'll drive."

As she brushed past him, though, her hand trailed against his elbow. It was only a light touch, but her fingers lingered briefly, and he felt electricity shoot up his arm.

He glanced at her, and she met his gaze. For a moment, neither of them looked away.

In the dingy, cold basement, there was no one around to see them.

The door was shut. Artemis was halfway to the exit but had paused, her hand still touching his arm.

For a moment, silence passed between them.

Then Forester leaned in, unable to resist, or at least unwilling. His breath blossomed against her cheek, but he didn't kiss her.

Rather, he leaned close.

It was a strange thing, he realized.

Talking of murder, of arrows, of money...

Not exactly romantic. And yet with Artemis, every moment was one full of romance. Not just the joys and the ecstasy and the pleasure, but the pain and the longing and the deep, yearning want.

And so the two of them stood close, neither of them retreating. He studied her mismatched gaze. One eye like cold frost, the other like molten gold. Both like precious stones.

Her fingers still against his arm, warm and inviting.

Was he misreading it?

Since when had he cared?

Now, he could feel his heart pounding, and he said, "God dammit, Artemis. I like you. Alright? You know it. But I really, really do. Shit, if I was good with words... I... I dunno... I might not have just said shit there. Who knows."

"Forester," she began, but he cut her off.

"No! No, let me say it. Let me finish. Okay? Yeah." He still was leaning close, still refusing to withdraw. She hadn't either.

It was as if time had suspended itself, as if everything had gone still.

"Look," he said firmly. "I loved her. My wife, I mean. I'd lie to you if I said I hadn't. And I won't lie to you. And when I first met you, yeah, you reminded me of her. You looked like her. But you are different than her. So different. And I love everything I've gotten to know about you."

"Forester!" she said. "Please!" There was a flash of something in her eyes. Was that guilt? Now, it was as if she couldn't quite meet his gaze.

But he soldiered on nonetheless. Emotions were fun, entertaining things that made him often think of a zoo. He could watch from behind bars, enjoy the view, but then retreat home whenever it grew too inconvenient.

Now, though, it was as if he'd jumped headlong out of a jeep on a safari, joining the pesky things in the heat and the sun.

He wasn't experienced with such feelings. Not really.

And so he spoke as he could, trying not to look like a lumbering idiot. "I care about you. More than anyone. I can't tell you what amount of my heart is still hers. But I can tell you that the amount I know how to give is yours. Alright? Shit—there you've made me go and say something sappy."

"Cameron," she said, still trying to cut him off.

"What?" he replied at last.

She hesitated, biting her own lip. "I... I've been lying to you."

He stared at her. Blinked. "Is... Are you still with Jamie?"

"No!" she said suddenly, eyes widening. "No, nothing like that."

He felt a flicker of relief, but it vanished quickly.

"Much worse," she whispered. "Much, much worse."

"What is it?" he said, still staring at her.

She was trembling now. He could see the way her fingers, pressed against her arm, were shaking. She looked scared.

Of him?

He hated that. He hated how much he scared her.

He tried to reach out, to hold her hand, but she withdrew. His knuckle brushed dark strands of hair from her eyes.

"My sister," Artemis whispered. "She's still alive." Artemis spoke in a still, quiet voice. A ghost of a whisper. A soft, sad, sweet voice.

Forester stared at her, his eyes hooded, unseeing and yet seeing.

"That's... that's really good news."

"No, it's not," Artemis protested. And now tears were welling in those beautiful eyes of hers. "She's the Ghost Killer, Forester."

Artemis blurted this part out as if it were taking everything in her just to say it. She winced as she did, shaking her head. The tears dripped down her face.

He rarely had seen her tear up. He wasn't sure if he'd ever seen her *really* cry. Perhaps once before.

Or was he just remembering *her*?

He shifted uncomfortably now.

"I don't understand."

"My dad's innocent," Artemis said. "And I know where he is. That CI from the last case? It was my dad, in disguise. I lied to you."

Forester blinked. He stared at her.

"Let me get this straight... Your sister is alive, but she's the real Ghost Killer? And you've been helping your dad hide?"

"Yes," Artemis said, her voice shaking horribly. "I'm so, so sorry for lying to you. But... But Helen, my sister, she's my best friend. I've been looking for her for decades. And... It's why Jamie left."

"Because you wouldn't turn your sister in?"

"Yeah."

Forester stared at her. Then, softly, he said, "I killed the man who killed my wife. I tracked him down. He hid out on some Podunk, no-name island. Thought for sure he was safe. But I found him. I ended him. Snuffed him out with my hands. Like a candle."

Artemis and Forester both stood in the dark, cold room now.

It was as if the room had grown bleaker. As if everything were colder. So cold that Forester felt shivers up his arms.

Artemis didn't look away.

He didn't look away from her. He found, strangely, having heard this burden she'd carried and now unleashed, that he didn't give two damns. He didn't care. If anything, he liked her more for it. She was loyal to her family. Loyalty.

Besides, people in glass houses couldn't throw hand grenades—or whatever the saying was.

Maybe it was just how intoxicating it was to stare at her. Maybe he was just having a moment. But he said, "I don't care about any of it, Artemis. I don't. I care about you. I know you did and do what you do because you think it's the right thing. Or at least because you're trying your best."

Artemis was still trembling. She didn't comment on what he'd told her. What she'd already inferred from her father's comments.

But it was as if she were willingly overlooking it. As if by not talking about it, she was letting him know that she was willing to look the other way.

Or maybe just forgive it completely?

He'd killed a man. And it didn't bother him. Not at all.

But what Artemis thought of him—now that caused his heart to ache.

It really was quite cold in the basement all of a sudden.

Perhaps it was this strange frigidity or just a childlike fear, but he suddenly moved in.

She didn't flinch. Didn't withdraw.

He wrapped his arms around her, holding her close. The warmth of their two bodies seemed to mingle.

They held one another close.

And Forester felt Artemis' tears against his cheek. Neither of them spoke, but they just held each other in the dark, in the cold, standing amidst the whispers and murmurs of shattered fears and burdens of guilt. But the pieces seemed smaller, less somehow.

And in that moment, the jagged bits of ice and debris, the remnants of hidden secrets, seemed to be melted away by the warmth of their touch.

And then she kissed him.

His mind was still moving, his arms still wrapped around her, when she drew back briefly.

He thought she was trying to pull away.

But instead, she'd been studying his lips and then moved in. Her eyes were still red-ringed. She looked even prettier when she cried, if such a thing were possible.

And she kissed him. Her lips against his, soft and gentle. He tasted the faintest touch of salt from a tear, but then it was washed away as they leaned into each other.

Neither of them withdrew. Neither of them wanted to. Their bodies pressed against each other, the warmth turning to something closer to kindled passion.

Forester deepened the kiss, his hands roaming over her body, feeling the curves and contours of her figure. She moaned softly, her hands tangling in his hair as she kissed him back with equal fervor. It was as if they were both letting go of everything that had held them back before and giving in to the moment.

The cold basement was now a distant memory, as their bodies pressed together, the heat between them intensifying with each passing moment. Forester lifted Artemis up, her legs wrapping around his waist as he carried her over to the table where they'd worked, facing the basement window. He laid her down gently, his lips trailing down her neck as he kissed her heatedly.

Artemis clung to him, her body arching against his as she gasped for breath.

Neither of them spoke. At least not with words, but in a way it felt like a song. A melody passing between the two of them.

For that moment, for those passing moments, it was as if all was right in the world.

And all Forester could hear was a shared music between him and the woman he cared about.

Thoughts of Bozeman arrows, of sordid murders, of billionaires and their wiles were distant things for the moment.

All that mattered was the proximity. The nearness.

The affection and the sensuality.

Neither of them stopped. Neither of them withdrew.

Things had changed between Artemis Blythe and Cameron Forester.

His heart felt weighty in his chest. Not *heavy* but weighty, substantive. As if he were feeling it again after a long, cold winter.

He knew darkness was coming. Deep darkness on the horizon. Violence, death, danger...

But for a while longer, he pushed it all from his mind.

CHAPTER 10

REVENGE WASN'T A DISH, nor was it best served cold.

Revenge was a coal, and the hotter it grew, the more it burned.

That's how the man in the golden robes saw things. Silly robes. A silly golden mask to match.

But those gathered in the large, opulent room took these things quite seriously.

And so he played his role.

Ten figures settled in chairs facing where he sat. Ten figures in dark suits and golden masks. All of them leaning forward, eager. He could *smell* the blood lust in the air.

He allowed himself a small, wicked smile. But no one saw it behind his mask.

He crossed his legs, then crossed his arms, causing the folds of his golden robe to cascade down his chest.

"Order!" he called out, clicking two perfectly manicured fingers together. "Order!"

The shuffling, the fidgeting, and the uncomfortable quiet continued. All eyes turned towards him now.

He spread his arms, all of a sudden, like a bird unfurling its wings to take to flight.

"We all know why we're here," he said softly. "Don't we?"

One by one, the men in the masks nodded. Two women as well, both sitting in the back, both watching.

One of the women was an awkward, unhinged thing. He'd grown to know her in country clubs and after-school encounters. She was a liability.

The other woman, sitting next to her, though, had bright, red hair.

This woman was a threat.

As cold as a crocodile's skin. Eyes like a shark's.

The liability was hunched over. The shark sat up straight.

His eyes moved on to the rest of the figures. Despite the suits, the hoods, the masks, he knew each of them by name.

For years he'd spent time with them. They'd grown to know each other, even befriend one another.

And then came the betrayal.

And then came the hunt.

"What are we waiting for?" one of the men called out. He had silver hair and wire-framed glasses visible behind his mask.

Reese Elwood operated one of the largest grocery market chains in the state. He also came from old money.

But he had a sniveling voice and whined most of what he said.

The leader just glared. Silence resumed.

He then said, "Our next hunt will take place tonight." He reached for an hourglass sitting in front of him. Then turned it slowly upside down.

Wide eyes stared at the grains of sand trickling through the hourglass, pooling in the bottom basin.

The leader watched as the sand continued to fall, his mind already on the hunt. He had been planning this for months, carefully selecting his prey and studying their every move. He had gathered information on their weaknesses and vulnerabilities, and he was ready to strike.

As the sand began to run out, the leader stood up and gestured for the others to follow. "We have work to do," he said, his voice commanding and authoritative. "Only a few of us have a kill."

Figures raised their hands at this part. Three of them. Three claiming the dead. Though he knew better. One of the victims had survived.

They would rectify that tonight.

"A repeat," he said slowly. "One that got away."

Shuffling now, discomfort.

He could see fear in their eyes.

Their biggest fears.

Fear that word had gotten out. That their reputations would be ruined. That someone would find out about these sordid games. Like children terrified that their parents had come home early.

But the leader was not afraid. He was in control. He had planned this hunt to perfection, and nothing would stand in his way.

His mind moved back to the start of all this. Planning had begun months ago, when he'd found out.

Found out what had been happening.

His eyes narrowed behind his mask, and he felt a white-hot rage flare through him.

The coal burned brighter.

He turned to the woman with the red hair, his eyes locking onto hers. "You will be my partner tonight," he said. She nodded, her expression betraying nothing.

The others rose from their seats, their masks concealing their expressions as they silently made their way out of the opulent room. The leader was the last to leave, the hourglass still in his hand.

He paused in the doorway, looking back. It was not the first time he had gathered these people together, nor would it be the last. But this time was different. This time, he had a score to settle.

He glanced at the hourglass, watching the last of the sand slip through his fingers. The time for revenge had come.

"Who's the target," the red-haired woman said at his side. "The new one is still in the woods."

"Not her," he replied softly. "Not yet. Soon... But our last kill wasn't a kill." He looked at the red-haired woman, holding her gaze, their masks expressionless.

"She's still alive?"

"Yes. But not for much longer."

And then he turned, his golden robes flourishing as he swept down the mansion's hall, leading the ten hunters in his wake.

CHAPTER 11

As THEY LEFT THE parking lot and strode up the concrete sidewalk to the warehouse, Artemis could tell things had changed with Forester.

But she tried to focus on the task at hand, ignoring the warm flush creeping to her cheeks every time he glanced in her direction.

Occasionally, he'd shoot her a self-satisfied smirk. She'd return a bashful smile. The two of them playing their roles, and yet even these were different now.

She'd told him the truth—told him about Helen—and he hadn't rejected her. Hadn't turned her in.

He'd simply understood.

And she understood him a bit better now, too.

The spell was broken, though, when Forester reached out and pressed the doorbell by the warehouse's rear entrance.

The two of them had come to a halt on the asphalt by the door, staring at the metal frame.

The ringing bell chirped a few more notes in the evening silence and then went quiet.

Above the door, it read *Distribution.*

The door opened a second later, and a chain rattled, keeping the door ajar.

A face peered out at them.

And then froze.

They stared back.

For a moment, it was as if time seemed to stand still.

The man's face was bruised. He was leaning heavily to one side as if favoring one leg. His head was shaved.

It was the skinhead from the shootout.

He was here...

"What the hell..." Artemis began.

The man opened his mouth to shout a warning over his shoulder, trying to fling the door closed, but Forester moved too fast.

He flung his massive frame into the door, snapping the chain and sending the door careening into the skinhead.

The man's shout turned to a strangled grunt, and he went reeling backwards into a dusty loading dock.

Forester followed quick, fist flying as he tackled the skinhead to the ground. Artemis stood frozen, watching the two men roll around in the dust, grunting and snarling like animals.

The skinhead was no match for Forester's brute strength, but he was surprisingly agile and managed to slip out of Forester's grasp a few times, landing a punch or a kick before Forester could pin him down again.

Finally, Forester got the upper hand, straddling the skinhead's chest and raining down blow after blow onto his face. Blood spurted from the skinhead's nose and mouth, and Artemis felt a sickening lurch in her stomach.

"Stop it!" she yelled. "Forester, stop!"

Forester paused, his fist poised for another strike. He looked up at Artemis, his eyes wild with adrenaline.

Artemis shook her head, hastening in the door; she tugged Forester's cuffs from his belt, handing them to the man.

He paused, glancing at her, blinking a few times, then down at the man who'd nearly killed them both.

As if this very thought crossed his mind; he snarled; struck the man a final time, knocking him unconscious; and then cuffed him.

He pushed to his feet now, shaking his head.

Artemis held a finger to her lips, though, peering into the expansive loading dock.

She spotted more than one bay, no trucks in sight. Stacks of boxes near metal racks that were empty.

Further back, through a doorway, she spotted a glowing light.

Forester hesitated, then slowly stood up, wiping his bloody knuckles on his jeans. The skinhead lay groaning on the ground, his face a swollen mess.

The man's leg was wrapped in a white cloth, bound tight. Blood showed through where he'd been shot back in the tunnel.

"The two others might be here," she whispered.

Forester paused, frowning then nodding.

Together, the two of them moved away from the unconscious man who occasionally groaned in his sleep.

The two of them moved along the tall, metal shelves. Occasionally, Artemis glanced along the shelves, searching for Bozeman arrows or any other clue.

Why was the shooter, who'd followed them then nearly killed them, hiding out at this warehouse?

Was he the source of the arrows?

Was she missing something?

They crept along silently, moving away from the empty, dusty loading dock, under high, metal rafters, towards the glowing light in the far w all.

The door was cracked open. But Artemis couldn't hear any sounds.

She shivered, half expecting a gunman to emerge from behind the door.

But as Forester eased the threshold open, there was no response. No sound.

Suddenly, Artemis froze, pointing. She hissed, and Forester glanced over.

He followed her gaze and stiffened. Her heart had skipped a beat, and her eyes were wide as she stared at a blinking camera above her, its lens glaring directly at her.

"They know we're here," she whispered.

Cameron took a running start, jumped, and snatched the camera off the wall, leaping nearly three feet into the air, and allowing his arm to reach ten feet above the floor.

He *thumped* back into the ground in a puff of dust, gripping the broken camera, wires jutting every which way where they'd been torn from the wall.

She swallowed.

"Can't see us now," Forester pointed out.

"Yeah. I understand the reasoning," she muttered. "Just not the methods."

"You weren't complaining about my methods a couple hours ago."

She blushed, and he gave her a quick kiss on the cheek.

She wasn't sure how she felt about this but didn't have time to react, as Cameron pushed through the metal door and slipped into the hall beyond.

Hesitantly, her stomach twisting, knowing that whoever was in here was expecting them, she followed. The hallway was dimly lit, and they moved slowly, cautiously. Artemis could hear her heart pounding in her ears. She kept close to Cameron, who'd drawn his weapon as if it were an extension of himself.

As they neared the end of the hallway, the light brightened, and they could hear the sound of voices.

They approached the door at the end of the hallway, and Forester motioned for her to take cover. She pressed herself against the wall, sweat prickling across her forehead.

From within, they could hear voices murmuring. One was saying, "You're sure? She was shot twice."

"I'm sure. They're going after her tonight."

"God dammit. We got enough shit to clean up without having to attack a damn hospital."

"Yeah, well, I don't make the rules, do I?"

Artemis frowned, staring at the door. Under her breath, so quiet she could barely hear herself speak, she whispered, "Are they talking about Whitney Martin? The girl we found this morning?"

Forester nodded, scowling. He tensed briefly.

Artemis stared, and then her eyes widened as she realized what he was about to do.

Forester kicked the door open and barreled into the room like some force of nature.

Artemis peered past him as he lunged inside.

The room was small and cramped, full of boxes and crates. There were two men inside, one of them bruised along the neck and face, the other a burly man with a thick beard.

The burly man cursed and reached for a weapon on the table in front of him, but Forester was too quick. He fired his gun, and the man fell to the ground, clutching his shoulder.

The second man stared at him, his eyes wide with fear.

"Get on the ground!" Forester yelled. "Now!"

The man hesitated, eyes twitching in his bruised face, but then he slowly lowered himself to the ground, hands up.

"Who are you working for?" Cameron snapped. "Hey—hey, you, answer me! Who are you working for? Who owns this place?"

Neither man spoke. The one shot in the shoulder groaned some more.

Artemis glanced around the room now that the threat was over. Forester was cuffing both men and dragging them out of the room, leaving her to temporarily search around.

She noticed a computer one of the men had been on—he'd left it logged in while reaching for his gun.

She approached the computer, careful to avoid the trail of blood on the ground.

She frowned, looking at the device and then murmuring to herself, "Let's see what we have here..."

She clicked along the links a for few moments, trying to reorient herself, and then found a page called *Shipping and Fulfillment.*

She followed this link to find *Private Acquisition.*

She hesitated, checking the other links next to it. One simply read *Frequency.* The other said *Tax Imp.*

She frowned and clicked on *Private Acquisition.*

Then, pressing Ctrl+F she searched for *Bozeman.*

She clicked return. Instantly, results appeared. She gave a low whistle, scanning the list of names that had acquired the expensive arrows from the place.

A few sporadic names recurred here and there, but mostly the list contained a single repeat client who ordered the arrows in bulk. More than a thousand arrows at a time.

She did some quick math, and her eyes widened further. Nearly a million dollars per shipment of arrows.

And yet multiple shipments.

"What the hell..."

She clicked the name on the arrow shipments and then went still.

Julius Bateman.

The man who'd hired them. Kayla's own father.

He'd been ordering the arrows. He'd offered them a hundred-million to find his daughter.

So why was his name associated with the arrows used to kill one of the other girls?

The same arrows that had been shot at Whitney, who was now recovering in the hospital.

Artemis glanced around the room, her heart racing.

Was she missing something? Why would Julius Bateman be buying the arrows used to kill his own daughter's friends?

Unless he wasn't buying them for himself...

Unless he was using them to track down whoever was responsible for his daughter's abduction.

He had the funds and the resources to be able to acquire the arrows, and he had the motive to want to track down the person responsible for his daughter's disappearance.

But why was he doing it in such a secretive manner? Who were the people he was working with?

Artemis took a deep breath, her mind whirring. She hesitated though, checking the dates of the purchases.

Before his daughter had gone missing.

So no. He hadn't ordered them to find the killers.

He'd ordered the murder weapons for some other reason.

She paused, frowning, and took a picture of the computer screen.

Then she turned, hastening back out into the hall to join Forester.

Chapter 12

Artemis stared up the winding path leading to the enormous mansion for the second time that day.

Forester was complaining as he drove, but she wasn't listening to much of it.

Still, his voice was fierce as he said, "Mum's the word. An hour. I wasted an hour with those assholes."

"They didn't say *anything*?" Artemis asked.

For the last hour, she'd sat out of the interrogation, preferring to double-check the orders of arrows she'd found.

She'd confirmed all the receipts went back to one name: Julius Bateman.

And they happened to be pulling into his enormous driveway.

Forester had spent an hour trying to interrogate the three men they'd found hiding out at the loading docks.

But they hadn't said a word.

"No IDs, no DNA, no fingerprints, nothing," Forester was saying. "How's that possible? How, in the 21st century, are three men just... *ghosts?*" he said, scowling. Then he winced, "Er, sorry."

She rolled her eyes. "I'm not offended by the word *ghosts,* Cameron."

"Oh, well... you know, just because your dad was called the—"

"No, I get it. It's fine."

"And your sister was—"

"Truly. It's fine." She hesitated, then realized he was teasing her. She scowled, reached out, flicked his ear, then emerged from the vehicle.

The gunmen weren't identifiable. But they now had a solid lead.

Forester joined her outside the car, the two of them standing in the shadow of the largest home either of them had likely seen.

The house looked like something out of a fairy tale, with its turrets and spires and ornate balconies. The lawn was perfectly manicured and the gardens were in full bloom, making the air smell of lavender and roses.

Artemis took a deep breath and walked up to the front door, her heart pounding in her chest. Forester lingered behind her. She glanced back at him, but he gave a quick nod.

She rang the doorbell and waited, her mind racing with questions.

Why had Julius Bateman ordered the arrows used to kill his daughter's friends? Was he working with someone else? And if so, who?

The door opened and a woman appeared, her eyes widening in surprise. The woman reminded Artemis of Agent Grant. She had silver hair, green, emerald earrings, and was wearing a beautiful gown that hugged her figure.

"May I help you?" the woman asked, her voice sweet and melodic.

"We're here to see Julius Bateman," Artemis said, trying to keep her tone steady. "It's urgent."

The woman hesitated, glancing between the two of them, but then nodded. "Please come in."

Artemis and Forester followed the woman through the grand entrance and into a spacious foyer. The walls were adorned with expensive paintings and sculptures, and the floors were made of gleaming marble.

"Wait here," the woman said, gesturing to a nearby sitting area. "I'll go inform Mr. Bateman of your arrival."

As soon as the woman disappeared, Artemis and Forester exchanged a look.

"Something's off," Artemis whispered. "Why would he order the arrows?"

Forester shrugged. "Maybe he's just a rich guy with a hobby."

Artemis rolled her eyes. "Highly doubtful."

They didn't have to wait long before the woman returned a few seconds later. She looked pale and flustered. She hesitated, cleared her throat, and then said, "I'm afraid Mr. Bateman can't meet with you."

"And why's that?" Artemis demanded.

"Because," the woman said quietly. She was shaking as she said it, her voice trying to maintain decorum. "He's dead."

CHAPTER 13

PARAMEDICS AND FORENSICS MOVED around the crime scene in the mansion, staring at the body on the bed.

Artemis shivered, her blood pumping faster as she stood in the doorway, watching as the crime scene was picked apart.

Evidence was bagged, and words were traded in hushed voices.

The man on the bed had three arrows protruding from his chest. In one hand, he gripped a rolled-up piece of paper, tinged blue with golden lines like a check.

His eyes were open, staring at the ceiling, and his face was twisted into a look of horror.

Artemis just stared at the man, trying to make sense of any of it.

"He must've killed himself," she murmured.

Cameron, standing in the hall next to her, said, "With arrows? Kinda hard, don't you think?"

"He could've hired someone to do it," she countered. "He's rich enough. Maybe he was trying to pay them." She nodded at the check.

Cameron just shrugged.

A man had paused by the bed, bent over, and retrieved a small pen, slipping it into a plastic evidence bag.

Artemis shook her head. "Are we sure that's really him? Maybe he faked his death. Money can buy all sorts of things. Even lookalikes."

"Nah," Forester said, tapping his phone. "Thumbprint is a match. DNA is a match. That's Mr. Bateman. There goes our leading suspect..." Then he added, "And probably our cash prize for finding his daughter."

"Which we haven't done yet," Artemis pointed out, her voice grim.

The two of them drifted off into silence, both of them sharing frowns.

Artemis tentatively moved into the room, avoiding the figures of two paramedics who were shaking their heads as they spoke with a police captain.

Artemis approached the bed, slowly, avoiding blood stains on the ground, and side-stepping where a forensic tech's camera had been left on the carpet.

She reached the bed, staring down.

The sight of blood didn't shock her how it used to. Death didn't scare her how it once had.

Bateman's eyes were open. Did people usually die with their eyes open?

She glanced to the window. It was unlocked.

Then back to the bed.

"No blood on the sheets," she murmured.

"What's that?" Forester said.

"No blood on the sheets," she repeated a bit louder.

"Huh. Body was moved here?"

"Posed here," she replied.

Forester reached out now, wearing a glove that he'd taken from a tech. He pried open the dead man's hand and withdrew the check.

The check was made out for fifty million dollars. And the name it was assigned to hadn't been filled in.

Forester whistled soft and slow. "Lotta cheese. Think he was trying to bribe someone? Maybe the kidnappers got to him. Ransoming Kayla."

Artemis paused then looked around. "Where's his phone?" she murmured.

"How's that?"

"His phone," she said, louder. "We need to find his phone."

Forester frowned, watching as Artemis began checking the night-stand, then he reached for the victim's pockets.

He shook his head. "Nothing."

Artemis winced, careful to avoid stains, then dropped to the ground, checking under the bed. "Empty," she said. "Nothing."

She was about to rise when she spotted something else.

Across the room, under the bed, she had a view of the closet.

The door to the closet was open, but on the ground, beneath a shoe box, a single floorboard was elevated higher than the rest.

CHAPTER 14

Artemis approached the elevated floorboard, frowning. A paramedic moved past her, wheeling a gurney. A coroner, one she didn't recognize, was speaking to two of the cops by the door.

Artemis though, focused on the floorboard. She stooped and pried at it, her fingers scrambling on the wood. She winced at a splinter but managed to pull the floorboard free.

And there, she spotted three items. A wad of cash. An old wedding ring. And a cellphone.

She reached for the phone, pulling it free.

Forester had joined her now, standing close.

"Huh. Nice find. Hunch?"

She shook her head, staring at the phone. "No... no, it just makes sense. His daughter was a pawn in his game."

"Hmm?"

She shook her head, waving a hand towards the bed. "The check he wrote. Fifty million? Someone was going to return his daughter, and for him, it would be like cutting a deal. Half off."

"And?"

"And," she said, "How did they contact him? How did they offer proof of life?"

Forester turned his attention back to the phone. Artemis had turned it on now and was frowning at the keypad requesting the passcode.

She hesitated then tried the address for the mansion.

The phone vibrated but remained locked. She considered it for a moment then tried three commas.

Still locked.

She frowned, glancing at Cameron.

"What's his daughter's birthday?"

Forester pulled out his own phone to check the information on Kayla Bateman.

Then he said, "March fifth."

Artemis entered *0305.*

The phone remained locked. She stared at the device, then glanced at the bed. She remembered how cavalier he'd seemed when they'd spoken to him. She closed her eyes in consideration. Then said, "What's *his* birthday?"

"April Eighteenth."

She entered 0418.

The phone unlocked.

She gave a little snort. "His birthday. Not his daughter's. His own."

Forester just glanced at the dead man on the bed, and Artemis felt bad for her temporary scorn.

She cycled through the phone, though, and arrived at recent messages.

Then she stopped.

"What's wrong?"

"Unknown number," she murmured. "It contacted him only a few hours ago." Forester glanced out the window at the darkening skies, his expression mirroring the horizon, his scowl deepening.

Her hand trembling, Artemis clicked on the text.

She read, softly, "*We have your daughter. Want her back? It'll cost.*"

"Is that all?"

"There's a link."

"Click it."

Artemis clicked the link in the text. The phone warned her that she was venturing outside safe websites, but she accepted the risk with a swiped of her thumb.

And then she heard heavy breathing.

A dark camera, a faint curse, then the sound of crunching footsteps. A whispering voice now, scrambled, garbled. A voice that was hard to understand because of the filters. But it was saying, in a whisper, "Julius, Julius... What should we do with her, hmm?"

The camera turned, aiming through the trees. And there, in the distance, Artemis spotted a young woman.

The girl was hiding behind a rocky outcrop, shivering, and clutching her arms against her shoulder.

Her shoulder was bleeding but had been bandaged by a soiled stretch of fabric.

The young woman clearly didn't see the videographer.

The man was still breathing heavily, hidden in the trees, still aiming the camera.

"Fifty mil," the voice said. "Two hours. Meet us at the cabin. If you don't come..." He pointed a gun in the direction of the girl, a hundred feet away. The voice then whispered, "*Bang.*"

Artemis stared as the image went still. She was breathing heavily, and Forester muttered, "Well, shit."

"They lured him out into the open," Artemis whispered.

"Then killed him?"

"Who leaves fifty mil," she said. "What's more important than fifty million?"

Forester's nose wrinkled now, contemplating this question. A cop was gesturing at them. The man by the door cleared his throat and said, "We need to empty the room, please."

Forester and Artemis began moving towards the door, the two of them both lost in their thoughts.

As they left, Forester said, "When I... found the man who killed my wife..." He hesitated, speaking so quietly, she had to lean in to hear. "He offered me money. A lot of it."

Artemis glanced at Cameron. He wasn't looking at her, and his teeth pressed tightly together.

"I wouldn't take it. No matter how much he offered."

She just watched him.

As they moved down a staircase, towards the exit to the mansion, Forester said, "The only things I can think of more valuable than fifty million are love... and revenge."

Artemis felt a faint shiver down her spine. She nodded as he said this.

But at this word *revenge.* Her heart skipped a beat. "Are the cops at the hospital yet?" she said quickly.

Forester blinked at the change in subject, but then he looked suddenly worried too. "For Whitney?"

"Yeah. That's who they're going after next. They're going to finish the job they started."

"You would think shooting a girl with two arrows was enough punishment," Forester muttered under his breath.

They pushed out of the ornate front door, and moved down the steps towards the waiting car, both moving quickly now.

"Two squad cars are outside the hospital. Two cops are on her floor," he said. "She's protected."

"Are we sure? If they can reach Julius, they can reach her too."

Forester frowned. "I mean... do you want to check on her?"

Artemis bit at the corner of her lip. Then said, "Maybe we can find them there. Maybe we can find something *useful.*"

"What about the drugs in our first victim's system? The fentanyl overdose."

"We can ask around about that at the hospital," Artemis said quickly. "Who better to know about a new illicit street substance than paramedics at the ER?"

"Fair point. To the hospital then. Also, it'll take some time, but I'll see if we can trace who sent that video file and message to Bateman's phone."

Artemis slipped into the car with Cameron, both of them lost in thought.

Dead end after dead end.

Julius had a check, but it was made out to no one.

Julius had been called, but the number had been blocked. It would take time to find out if they could track the number. The gunmen they'd captured at the warehouse were ghosts. No ID, no DNA evidence, nothing.

They needed to find something. Some lead or clue.

Or another girl would die.

Now, it seemed unlikely they'd be paid for the job. But that didn't matter to Artemis anymore.

Someone was getting away with murder. Someone with connections, wealth, power...

And it was her job to find out who was behind all of it.

CHAPTER 15

AT NIGHT, THE HOSPITAL resembled a dark bruise against the skyline. The moon was out, but clouds had swirled in, cutting off the lunar glow.

Artemis strode along the parking lot, checking cars, and searching for any motion.

For nearly an hour, she'd been patrolling the parking lot with Forester, the two of them searching for anything untoward.

Now, she paused by a jeep, peering into the back seat.

Empty.

A parking permit dangled from the window. She shivered briefly, moving on to the next car. Further down, she spotted Cameron's silhouette where he also moved from car to car, checking each one.

She paused briefly near a concrete barrier, looking out through a windowless opening at the hospital. Glowing orange lights illuminated the building, casting eerie shadows across the parking lot.

Suddenly a sound caught her attention. Artemis spun around as she scanned the area.

Footsteps. Heavy, rushed footsteps.

She saw a figure running towards her, and her heart rate skyrocketed.

"Hey!" she called out, hand still hovering near her gun. "Stop right there!"

The figure slowed, then stopped, panting heavily. He was wearing a headband and a smartwatch, which he'd been checking as if he hadn't seen her standing there.

Artemis approached cautiously, her eyes scanning for any signs of danger.

As she got closer, she recognized the figure as a young man, probably in his early twenties. He was sweating profusely, and his eyes widened in fear as she approached.

"What are you doing here?" Artemis demanded.

"I... I was just visiting my friend," the young man stammered. "She's in the hospital. I swear."

Artemis eyed him suspiciously, but something about his fear seemed genuine.

"Which room?" she asked.

The young man pointed towards the hospital. "Room 315," he said.

She noticed the line on his heartbeat monitor was pulsing. His shirt was stained in sweat.

He stammered, "I... I sometimes go for runs at night," he said quickly. "When she's sleeping. If she's awake I like to be there for her, but..." He trailed off, shaking his head. "Are you with those new security guys?"

She paused, her hand raised as she had been gesturing for him to continue.

"What security?" she asked.

He blinked. "Oh. Sorry. Never mind then."

"No, hang on," she cut in quickly. "What security?"

She glanced over at Forester who was approaching them now.

"Anything?" Forester asked. He glanced at the jogger.

The young man twisted at his sweatband, looking uncomfortable now.

"He was just telling me about new security," Artemis said, looking back towards the man. "*What* security?" she repeated.

"The—the new guys," he stammered. "The ones who came to the back entrance. A nurse let them in."

Artemis felt a cold chill run down her spine. "These new guys—how many of them were there?"

"Umm... Like five?" He stared at her, then glanced at Forester and back again. "Is—is everything okay? Is the hospital safe?" he said suddenly, turning to look back at the building.

He seemed too genuine to be faking. Artemis was beginning to trust he was telling the truth, but now, her fears were rising.

"When did this new security team show up?" she said quickly. "What did they look like?"

"Umm. About ten minutes ago, I think?"

"And what did they look like?" Forester said, emphasizing the question.

"I-I'm not sure. They were wearing black suits and had these earpieces in. They looked like they meant business."

Artemis cursed under her breath. "Forester, we need to get inside. Now."

They hastened away, moving towards the concrete stairs in the back of the parking structure. As they rushed towards the entrance, Artemis tried not to think about what they might find inside. She had a bad feeling in the pit of her stomach, and the hairs on the back of her neck were standing on end.

When they reached the back entrance, they saw that it was slightly ajar. Forester gestured for her to stay back, and he moved ahead, his gun drawn. She could hear his footsteps on the linoleum floors, and then there was silence.

"Forester?" she called out softly.

No answer.

Artemis took a deep breath and stepped inside, her fingers twitching against her thigh. The hallway was empty, but she could hear the sound of footsteps coming from one of the rooms. She crept forward, her heart pounding in her chest.

As she reached the door, she heard the sound of someone whimpering. She pushed it open and saw a nurse lying on the ground, her face contorted in pain.

Cord was wrapped around her wrists.

Artemis rushed to her side, checking for a pulse. She was alive, but barely. "What happened?" she asked, but the nurse was too discombobulated to answer. She was bleeding from where she'd evidently been struck over the forehead.

She heard footsteps again and turned to see Forester walking towards her. He was moving quickly and holding a finger to his lips.

She went quiet.

He pointed over his shoulder and mouthed the word *stairs*. Then held up two fingers.

Artemis glanced back at the nurse, then towards a first aid kit on the wall. She snatched the kit, grabbed gauze scissors from within, and cut the bindings around the nurse's wrists.

She then whispered, quietly, "Can you tend to your own wound? Someone is in danger."

The woman blinked, disoriented.

"Which floor is Whitney Martin being kept on?" Forester asked.

The nurse looked confused.

"The one shot with arrows," Artemis provided.

The nurse blinked and then said, "Third floor."

Artemis paused and then winced. She wondered now if the jogger was one of Whitney's friends.

Forester was still holding a finger to his lips though. He gestured at Artemis, and as Artemis double-checked the nurse was alright, the two of them crept back into the hall, moving quietly.

At the far end, Artemis spotted the two shadowy figures Forester had been indicating.

Both of them standing at the base of the stairs, framed between two faux plants. Both of them clutching heavy weaponry.

"We have to go quietly," Forester whispered. "Distract them. If the others hear gunshots..."

She nodded. Five attackers. That's what the jogger had seen.

Only two here, which meant three were moving up the stairs now. What if it was too late for Whitney?

Artemis cursed, glancing around desperately.

Her eyes landed on a fire extinguisher mounted on the wall nearby. She looked back at Forester and nodded towards it. It wasn't a very *good* plan. In fact, it wasn't much of a plan at all.

But for the moment, they had to hurry. Whitney's life hung in the balance.

Artemis grabbed the fire extinguisher and heaved it down the hallway with all her might. It crashed against the wall, making a loud noise that echoed through the empty halls.

The two attackers spun around, their weapons at the ready. Forester then charged them both, slamming into them from behind with a grunt, knocking one of the guns to the ground and sending the other skidding away. He took a few hits but kept going, his arms extended, ready to grapple with them.

He lunged at the first gunman, striking him in the chest with the force of a moving truck.

Before the man could make a sound, Forester slammed a fist into his throat.

Then, while the man gurgled for air, Forester grabbed his arms and wrestled him to the ground.

The second man tried to strike Cameron from behind, but Forester was already moving.

While still holding onto the first man's arm in a lock, Cameron rolled onto his back, using his legs to grip the second man's shoulders, rendering him immobile.

He squeezed with his legs, locking them into a triangle.

One man was pressed under Forester's body weight, arm trapped. The other was being choked out by Cameron's legs.

It had all happened in a matter of seconds.

Artemis hastened forward, snatching the fire extinguisher off the ground.

As she turned towards the stairs again, she glimpsed a flash of silver.

The man who was still standing, being choked by Cameron's legs, was desperately grappling at his belt, pulling forth a knife.

He raised it to bury it into Cameron's leg.

Artemis yelped in surprise, and her instincts took over.

She flung the fire extinguisher a second time.

The metal cylinder flew through the air, hitting the man square in the face. He stumbled backwards, dropping the knife as he fell. Forester quickly disarmed him, picking up the weapon and tossing it aside.

The first man was unconscious now, though, she hadn't seen it happen.

The second only lasted a moment longer before Forester's elbow found his temple.

Then he dropped to the ground as well.

Artemis breathed a sigh of relief, then glanced up the stairs, wondering what they would find on the third floor.

She didn't have to wonder for long.

They couldn't hesitate.

Side by side, Cameron and Forester rushed silently up the stairs.

No gunshots. No screaming.

Not yet.

CHAPTER 16

HE WATCHED FROM THE top of the parking structure, like a king looking over his domain. He was quiet, he was attentive, and he was vengeance.

He stared down at the parking structure, his features hidden by his mask, his gloved hands pressed lightly together, his fingers touching.

He stood in a contemplative posture, and then asked, softly, "Are they in yet?"

The woman at his side nodded once. Her red-hair cascaded down her shoulders, framing her golden mask. He eyed the soft flesh of her neck and felt a longing deep within.

But he tore his gaze away.

He was a man of self-control. The same couldn't be said for others.

"Did he sob? Did he cry?" the woman asked softly.

"Hmm?"

"Julius."

A smile. She couldn't see it, but she likely heard it in his voice. "He wept as he died. He felt every ounce of pain."

"Do they know what we did to him?"

"No. They don't. Why should they?"

The woman made a purring sound. Her fingers resting on his shoulder, her body warm against him as she drew close. She slipped her hand inside his jacket, her hand now against his chest.

He felt a shiver of pleasure course down his spine. His breath came slowly.

"Not here," he murmured.

The woman chuckled but didn't listen. Her hand moved up to his hair, stroking the back of his head and tweaking the strap of his mask.

"We should be down there for this," she said.

"No. Not yet. Not now. Not until we find the others. Then."

"Then," she said.

The two of them stood in silence, overlooking the hospital, both of them watchful and vigilant and simmering with both rage and passion.

The woman's hand lingered on his shoulder, and her voice was soft as she whispered in his ear. "I'm sorry about what happened. I'm sorry for how this all started."

He tensed, his shoulders tight.

No one else was around to see them. The others were down in the hospital, completing the hunt.

Fools. All of them fools. All except *her*.

"I'm very, very sorry for your loss."

His mind fluttered, moving to other memories. He thought of what he'd lost. A wilted flower. Trampled under the feet of evil.

And here he was, the typhoon sent by God to level Sodom.

He was a hard man. A deadly man. People had died under his hands. The things he'd done to Julius Bateman?

Not worth repeating in polite company.

But now, with no one else to see him except the red-haired woman, he began to shake.

Tears appeared in his eyes. His shoulders trembled, and he let out a strangled gasp.

"Shh, shh," she whispered. "It's going to be okay. It's all going to be over soon."

He continued to tremble. Tears spilled down his face, slipping against the grooves in his mask.

He exhaled a few times, hyperventilating.

The red-haired woman held him tight, her fingers rubbing circles on his back. He felt her warmth, her comfort, and in that moment, he knew that she was the only one who truly understood the weight of his burden.

"I can't do this anymore," he whispered, his voice choked with emotion.

"Yes, you can," she replied firmly. "We're so close now. We can't stop."

He pulled away from her, turning his back to her as he tried to regain his composure. He wiped the tears from his face, his breaths coming in short gasps.

"You don't understand," he said, his voice low and raw. "It's not going to change anything."

The woman stepped closer to him, her hand once again resting on his shoulder. "It isn't about change. It's about justice."

He turned back to face her, his eyes red and swollen. "But at what cost?"

"At the cost of everything," she said firmly. "At the cost of making sure that those who deserve punishment receive it. You know as well as I do that the law can't always do what needs to be done."

He nodded slowly. He inhaled a few more times. And then he was back to normal.

The flashes of emotion were rarer nowadays, but still raw.

He stood tall once more, straight-backed, staring down at the hospital, eyes narrowed.

And that's when he heard the gunshots.

CHAPTER 17

ARTEMIS AND FORESTER CREPT along the hospital halls, both of them keeping low. Artemis could feel her skin prickling, anticipation building as the two of them pushed through a glass door leading into the third-floor ICU.

The door was unlocked.

That was the first bad sign.

The second was the nurse lying dead on the ground by two overturned wheelchairs where she'd evidently slipped while trying to escape.

Artemis stared in horror at the scene before her. The room was empty aside from the nurse's lifeless body and the overturned wheelchairs. The silence was deafening, and Artemis felt a knot form in her stomach. She had a sinking feeling that they were too late.

Forester, ever vigilant, motioned for her to stay put as he crept forward, gun drawn. Artemis watched as he disappeared through the doorway leading to the next room. Her heart pounded in her chest.

Seconds felt like hours as she waited, ears straining for any sound. And then she heard it—a muffled scream, followed by the sound of a struggle. Without a second thought, Artemis charged forward.

She found Forester in the next room, his gun trained on a man holding a young nurse hostage. The man's eyes were wild, his grip on the nurse tight. The man was wearing a black outfit with a radio on his belt. He kept reaching towards the radio but stopped whenever Forester growled.

"Keep your hand away from that. Drop the gun!" Forester snarled, his voice firm and commanding.

The man had wide eyes and silver hair along his temples. He hesitated for a moment, eyes flickering between Forester and Artemis. And then he made his move. In one swift motion, he jammed his own weapon against the nurse's temple.

"Who the hell are you?" the man snarled, glaring at the two of them.

Forester kept his own gun aimed high.

Artemis froze, her mind racing as she tried to come up with a plan. She could see the fear in the nurse's eyes, the desperation in the man's.

He was clearly scared. A momentary pause. Everyone went still, eyes wide, searching.

It was as if instinct took over. Forester had different instincts. The sort that told him to punch or kick or charge or yell.

Artemis, on the other hand, went still. Quiet.

She observed.

For a brief moment, it almost felt like only two people were in the room.

The gunman. And her.

It was as if the pieces were all there. The woman—the queen—being threatened. Forester a bishop, ready to be sent into battle.

White to move, checkmate in one.

The clock was running down.

Artemis' subconscious pieced together the information rapidly.

Gray hair on his temples. Fear in his eyes. He'd drifted from the other attackers. Where were they?

Irrelevant.

She discarded the information as quick as thought, her mind moving a million miles a minute.

Unlike most, Artemis thought in chains of mental energy. Instead of following a linear path from point A to B, her mind would think of A, and then in a split second, process Z. All the points in between would be covered with lightning-fast calculation.

It wasn't anything conscious she did—it was simply how her brain worked.

The fear in his eyes was the weakness. The finger tensed on the gun. The nurse held as hostage. His hands trembling. He didn't want to be here.

He wanted a way out.

This man would do *anything* for a way out.

He didn't look like a killer. His fingers were soft—the hands of someone who had never labored a day in their life.

His suit was expensive.

His shoes gave him away. Multi-thousand-dollar shoes. The types of shoes she'd never worn in her life.

This was a very wealthy man.

And so she made her play.

All these thoughts crossed her mind in an instant, and she reached a decision.

"Fifty grand each," she said suddenly. "And we'll let you go."

The man blinked.

Forester shot her a hesitant glance.

Of course, Artemis was bluffing. But the funny thing about the wealthy: some of them used their finances to solve every problem.

She'd once heard a professional author mention how he had hired movers to help his neighbors pack up boxes and move into a new home.

Instead of showing up, instead of being neighborly and sacrificing his energy and time, he'd used money.

Most hadn't found a problem money couldn't solve.

Of course, Artemis had met just as many awful people in *all* income brackets.

But it was about finding *what type* of weakness someone manifested.

She repeated herself, louder, giving him a timer, giving him a sense of urgency. "Now it's a hundred grand each. Keep stalling and it's no deal at all."

"Who are you?" the man said, stammering.

She shook her head. "That's not how this works."

Her voice was like steel, though her heart was ricocheting inside her chest.

The man hesitated for a moment, his eyes darting between Artemis and Forester before finally settling on the gun he held. The seconds ticked by, the tension in the air almost palpable.

Finally, the man seemed to make a decision. With trembling hands, he slowly lowered the gun, his eyes never leaving Artemis. "Deal," he said, his voice barely above a whisper.

Artemis felt a flood of relief wash over her, but she didn't let it show. Instead, she kept her expression neutral as she said, "Now lower the gun."

He hesitated, swallowing.

"How do I know you're going to keep your side of the deal?"

She took a step to the right.

She had him hooked. Had his full attention. *This* was the goal.

Now, he made the fatal mistake. His eyes tracked her, wide and hopeful. He stared at her, desperation in his gaze.

She said, "You can't. I won't."

He frowned. "Wh-what?"

And then Forester, who had stepped the other way as Artemis had stepped right, moved in fast.

He was a blur. Just off to the left of the shooter. The man with the gun hesitated too long. He'd lost track of Cameron. The sound alerted him, and he swiveled sharply.

But he moved in time to bring his head on a collision course with the butt of Forester's handgun.

Crack!

The man staggered back, his legs going limp like strands of pasta.

Artemis watched as the man crumpled to the ground, unconscious. She let out a breath she didn't even realize she was holding. Forester moved quickly, checking the man's pulse before turning to Artemis with a nod.

"Nice work," he said, his tone laced with both relief and admiration. "I didn't think that would work."

Artemis shrugged, trying to hide the fact that her hands were shaking. "It was worth a shot."

They both looked around the room, taking in the chaos that had preceded their arrival. Broken glass littered the floor, overturned cots and medical equipment. And the nurse had ducked behind one of the beds, hiding from sight. Artemis felt a twinge of guilt for not immediately consoling the nurse, but she was relieved to see that she was unharmed.

"It's okay!" Artemis called out softly. "We're FBI. It's going to be okay."

"There are more of them!" the voice whispered from behind the cot. "Two others with guns! They're down the hall! I wouldn't let them in so I locked myself in here. But he broke down the door."

Her eyes peered out, glowing from behind the cot, and her voice trembled as she spoke.

Forester gestured towards the door. "We should hurry." In the direction of the cot, he added, "Ma'am the police are on their way. Just stay here, okay? Stay hidden!"

The two glowing eyes bobbed as the woman nodded her head.

Forester then took off again, leaving the unconscious man on the ground. Artemis looked back and said, "Please tie him up. Make it secure."

The nurse blanched but nodded.

Then Artemis followed Cameron out of the room and down the hallway. They emerged into a dimly lit side passage, and Artemis couldn't help but feel the prickle along her skin as they moved down the empty hall.

Everything seemed quiet again.

Where were the two other gunmen?

Where was Whitney's private room?

They glanced through windows as they moved. But most of the ICU beds were empty.

Artemis could feel her pulse racing as she followed Forester through the seemingly vacant hospital. The lights were off, save a faint flickering coming from the end of the hall.

A janitorial closet was open off to Artemis' left, and she spotted a hastily discarded mop, and a thin glaze of soapy water having pooled on the ground where the bucket had toppled.

No sign of a janitor. No sign of anyone at all.

Suddenly, Forester caught her arm, and she nearly jumped out of her skin. He pointed to a door at the far end of the hall. The door was closed, and something was blocking the window, concealing whatever was inside from view.

Artemis frowned.

The two of them moved towards the door, silent, avoiding the spilled pool of soapy water.

They reached the door, both breathing quietly.

Forester reached out, the door handle moving slowly where he pressed down.

Artemis could feel her heart hastening. Could feel her mind in tumult.

Forester eased the door open, and the two of them were suddenly assailed by a sudden gust of cold wind. Artemis shivered as the cold wind whipped around her, raising goosebumps on her skin. She squinted her eyes against the sudden brightness, as a light shone directly in her face. Blinking rapidly, she tried to adjust her eyes to the pointed, LED flare, and slowly the room came into focus.

It was a large, open space, with low ceilings and concrete walls painted white. The only source of light came from a large, industrial lamp hanging from the ceiling, illuminating the room in a harsh, white glow. Artemis could see the outline of several large objects in the center of the room, and her curiosity got the better of her.

She took a tentative step forward, and as she did, a voice boomed from the shadows.

"Stop right there."

Artemis froze, her heart pounding in her chest.

"Who are you?" the voice demanded.

Artemis's heart pounded. She couldn't see the source of the voice. No gunshots. No bullets.

Forester hadn't fired either, suggesting he didn't find the voice to belong to a threat just yet.

Across the room, she spotted a wide open window. Half the glass was smashed, littering the ground.

There was an empty bed in one corner. A toppled electrical machine.

The items in the center of the room proved to be an overturned defibrillator and a gurney.

The voice was coming from behind the defibrillator. She spotted a figure hunched there, breathing heavily. His one hand was clutching at his shoulder.

He had short-cut hair and was bent double as if trying to hide his form.

She cleared her throat. "FBI," she said slowly. "Who are you?"

The moment she said it, the man behind the toppled machine let out a faint breath of relief, but just as quickly, he hesitated.

She could see in his straightening and sudden slouch the suspicion washing over him.

"Show me a badge?" he snapped.

"Who are you?" Forester called back, his gun trained on the spot. "What happened in here? Where are the others?"

But the man just shook his head. "Badge, now!"

"Who are you?" Forester repeated, his voice growing more firm.

"Hospital security!" the man snapped. He raised a badge of his own, waving it over his head, the small, glinting thing catching the glowing lights above.

Artemis felt another flutter of relief, but fear quickly followed. Where was Whitney?

Where were the two other shooters?

"Now show me your damn badge!" barked the security guard.

Forester glanced at Artemis, and she gave a quick nod.

He pulled his badge from his pocket and tossed it across the room.

The security guard caught it with a single hand, his eyes scanning over the badge carefully. After a long moment, he finally seemed to be satisfied, and he relaxed his grip on his wounded shoulder.

Artemis nodded, but her mind was still racing. "What about the other shooters?" she asked. "Did you see anyone else in here?"

The security guard shook his head. "Got shot at. They went out the window."

"Hang on," Forester said quickly, holding up a hand and frowning. "*Who* went out the window?"

"I was making my rounds when I heard something in here, and when I came in, I saw the window was broken and the machines were over-turned. I thought we had a break-in, but I didn't see anyone. Then some asshole takes a shot at me."

He winced again, shifting and groaning. Then, he slowly stood to his feet, giving them a good look at him.

A tall, muscled man with a thin chinstrap and salt-and-pepper hair. He was glancing at them both nervously.

And Artemis finally noticed something. His eyes kept shifting, moving as if attempting to push out the side of his face.

He was glancing again and again towards the overturned bed, flaring his eyes, his nostrils.

Forester opened his mouth as if to speak, confused, but Artemis caught his arm, holding him. Forester went quiet.

She noticed, now, the tense way the guard was standing. The strange flow of his words, as if he'd rehearsed chunks of some monologue.

The fear and desperation in his voice when they'd first entered the room. Not directed at them, though.

The relief when they'd announced who they were.

But then the sudden suspicion... Perhaps not suspicion but more fear.

The sort of fear that occurred when faced with imminent danger. He kept shooting glances towards the toppled bed.

And now, as Artemis stared at it, she thought she spotted the faintest shifting of a shadow.

A murmur of a voice.

The window was still smashed. The glass scattered everywhere.

But someone was behind the bed.

More than one someone?

There were two gunmen still at large.

She nudged Forester, nodding towards the bed now.

From the angle where the security guard stood, she guessed that whoever was behind the bed could see him. Perhaps even aiming a gun at his spine.

She supposed he'd been threatened. If he said anything that warned them, he'd be shot.

So now, facing them, he had settled for widening his eyes, flaring his nostrils.

He looked silly, but the tension in the room stoppered any potential smile.

Forester was now creeping slowly forward, his own gun in hand.

It was moments like these that made Artemis wish she had a weapon of her own.

Another shifting shadow.

Two figures behind the toppled bed, crouched low. Likely both armed.

Forester was approaching quietly. He hesitated as he drew near, keeping in a straight line so that he could avoid being spotted.

Then, he lowered his shoulder, tensed, and flung himself at the bed.

He slammed into the toppled bed, sending it careening into the two figures using it as cover.

Both men behind the bed shouted in alarm. There was a gunshot, and debris trickled from the ceiling.

The bed slammed both men into the wall behind them, like a sandwich press.

Their shouts of surprise turned to grunts as the breath was knocked from their lungs.

One man tried to aim over the bed, but Forester knocked his gun away.

The man snarled and, groaning, managed to claw his way over the cot, slipping up between the wall and the bed. His shoulder hung strangely, an arm limp. Had he broken it?

It didn't matter. The man was wearing dark clothing and a golden chain around his neck.

He snarled as he flung himself at Cameron and sent the two of them toppling to the ground.

Artemis watched in horror as Forester wrestled with this gunman, their bodies rolling across the floor.

But the second gunman had now extricated himself from the wall. And was stooping to pick up his own weapon.

He winced as he bent double, listening to the snarls of the wrestling man.

But the gunman was now raising his own weapon.

Artemis needed to act fast. She scanned the room for anything she could use as a weapon and spotted a bed pan.

She snatched the metal item, took two steps forward, and began to swing.

The gunman raised his weapon.

Clang!

She struck first.

The bedpan ricocheting off his skull.

The man stumbled back, dazed, and Artemis took the opportunity to grab the gun that had fallen from his hand. Her hands trembled as she gripped it, but some small amount of instinct kicked in—the instincts Forester had been attempting to give her. She aimed the weapon at the man, ready to fire if he made any sudden moves. But he just lay there, groaning in pain.

Meanwhile, Forester had managed to pin down the other gunman. He was struggling to keep the man's weapon hand under control. Artemis rushed over to help, pointing her gun at the man's head.

"Drop the gun," she yelled.

The man hesitated, but with Forester's help, they managed to disarm him. Artemis breathed a sigh of relief.

"Who are you working for?" Forester demanded, his voice low and menacing.

The men remained silent, refusing to speak.

"Who sent you?" Forester snapped.

Both men remained silent. The one Artemis had struck was massaging his head gingerly, his fingers coming away with blood.

The second man was wheezing on the ground where Forester kept him pinned with a knee.

"Who hired you?" Forester demanded a third time.

Artemis cut in, "Where's Whitney?"

One of the men flinched, half glancing towards the window then hurriedly looking away again.

Artemis turned, looking at the smashed window as well.

She felt a slow shiver... She hastened to the window, stumbling forward, peering out.

Some of the glass had fallen on the other side of the window as well. In fact, most of the glass was outside.

Someone had broken it from the inside.

Whitney Martin had escaped again.

Artemis felt a rising sense of awe at what the young woman was willing to do to stay alive.

Shot with two arrows, she'd stumbled out of the woods.

And now, gunmen had come for her in the hospital but she had smashed a window and escaped.

But how?

Artemis frowned, looking around. The top of the hospital building was too tall. There was nowhere for Whitney to run. No visible stairs or ladder.

Artemis turned back to the room, her mind racing. If Whitney had escaped, then she was still in danger. They needed to find her before the gunmen did.

"We need to get out of here," she said to Forester, who was still pinning down the second gunman.

Forester nodded and stood up, pulling the man with him. "Tie them up," he snapped, pointing at the security guard.

The guard nodded quickly, hastening forward and snatching one of the guns from the ground. Artemis suspected the guard's own weapon was empty.

Forester made sure the bonds on the two men were tight before he hastened towards the door with Artemis.

Artemis nodded, grabbing the bedpan again just in case. They made their way out of the room. As they walked down the hallway, Artemis kept her eyes peeled for any sign of movement.

They reached the elevator and Forester pressed the button. As they waited, Artemis heard a faint noise coming from one of the rooms nearby. She motioned for Forester to follow her, and they crept towards the sound.

It was a small bathroom, and the door was slightly ajar. Artemis peeked inside and went still.

CHAPTER 18

WITHIN THE BATHROOM, THE window was smashed. This time, a large amount of glass lay *inside* the room.

Someone had come along outside and then entered again.

Now it made sense.

Whitney had escaped through one window, found there was no way down, moved along the roof, and entered back into this small, dark bathroom...

And then she'd never left.

Artemis' eyes widened as she spotted the shadowy figure cowering near one of the stalls. Wide eyes stared out at them.

Whitney huddled in the corner, her breath coming in frightened gasps.

"Whitney!" Artemis rushed forward. "FBI! We're FBI!"

Whitney seemed to recognize them both, and she nodded, unable to speak it seemed. Her chest was wrapped in white bandages, and she was wearing a loose hospital gown.

Tears streamed down her face. She managed to stutter the word, "G-g-guns."

"We got them," Forester cut in quickly, his voice low. "They're not going to hurt you. We had them tied up."

Whitney stared in relief, tried to rise to her feet, but then wobbled briefly.

"Are you... are you really FBI?" she asked, leaning against a bathroom wall.

"I am," Forester cut in. "You're looking a bit better."

Whitney winced, still leaning against the stall. She was breathing in and out slowly.

At first, Artemis inched forward, scared the woman might pass out. But then Whitney breathed a bit easier, a hand to her chest.

Artemis glanced over her shoulder nervously.

"We should wait until the police arrive," she whispered.

Forester nodded, keeping the door closed, and bracing his foot against it.

They'd cleared the hospital, but there was no point in taking risks. And for the moment, Whitney looked as if she was on enough pain meds to manage.

"I'm... I'm recovering," she whispered slowly. She grimaced. "The morphine is doing its job." She snorted. "Not the strongest thing I've ever tried, but still..."

She tried to chuckle but then winced.

Forester gave an appreciative nod at the humor in the face of pain, but Artemis was frowning, her mind racing.

"Did you... have you ever tried fentanyl?"

Whitney paused, wincing. She glanced between the two FBI agents.

"We aren't DEA," Artemis said quickly. "We don't care what you ingest. I just need to know if you had any idea that Marcy Thomas was on fentanyl."

Another long pause. Whitney slowly slid, leaning against a paper towel dispenser.

"She was a friend of yours, wasn't she?" Artemis pressed.

Whitney's face was pale, and Artemis wasn't sure if this was due to blood loss or a sudden bout of fear.

She hesitated briefly, then murmured, "Marcy... sometimes liked to party. Why?"

"There was a special blend of fentanyl in her system. A hybrid drug. Do you know what she was on? Who provided it to her?"

Whitney shook her head firmly.

Forester cut in now. "Are you sure you don't know who did any of this?"

Whitney shook her head adamantly. Her voice seemed to be weakening now, and she was leaning back.

Artemis could hear sirens now. Could hear voices coming from further down the halls.

But her attention was fixated on Whitney. The young woman gathered herself and said, "It's like I told the officers. I didn't see the people who attacked me. I don't remember what happened in the woods."

She shrugged and then winced, breathing slowly, her face like a ghost's.

Artemis glanced at Forester, holding out a hand behind her back as if to say *she's had enough.*

The two of them went quiet, listening to the sound of boots on the stairs. Voices in the halls.

Backup had arrived.

"Clear!" a voice called.

"We're in here!" Forester called out. "Agent Forester. FBI! Don't shoot!"

There was a flurry of movement as the police made their way towards them, footsteps thumping against the ground, the tapping of metal barrels against kevlar vests.

Suddenly, a hand gripped Artemis'.

She glanced over and realized Whitney had come in close. She whispered softly now, her voice shaking, "Marcy was really smart. She might've made the pills herself."

Artemis frowned at Whitney. The young woman was breathing heavily as if the words were taxing her. But she pressed on, still whispering even as the bathroom door flung open and flashlights shone in. Police congregated in the door, shouting out instructions.

But Whitney was speaking rapidly now, "Marcy was dating someone at the time. Someone she shouldn't have been seeing. She wouldn't tell me who. I think it was dangerous. I *think*."

"Do you know a name? Any idea who it might've been?"

A frown, a shake of the head. "No. But I know the two of them would meet out of town where no one knew them. There's a small bar on the highway leading south. It's called *Biggie's Small.*"

Police now streamed into the room. Paramedics followed.

Whitney seemed to lose her strength now, slumping as two paramedics reached her. In a small voice, her tone pleading, she said to Artemis, "Please find who did this."

And then she was led away by the paramedics, leaving Artemis with a knot in her stomach and a scowl on her face.

CHAPTER 19

NIGHT HAD FALLEN COMPLETELY as their car pulled into the parking lot outside *Biggie's Small,* and Artemis could feel her pulse quickening.

Forester stared at the small bar set on the side of the highway near an old gas station.

"This is where Whitney said Marcy Thomas used to come?"

Artemis nodded once.

"What are we gonna find here? Whoever she was dating isn't going to keep coming."

Artemis shrugged. "Maybe someone remembers her. Recognizes her. It's not like any of the shooters are talking."

Forester frowned. The two of them both had been advised that everyone arrested at the hospital had immediately lawyered up as well.

The lawyers who'd arrived had all been extremely expensive.

Money was behind all of this. And Artemis was beginning to feel like this town bled currency.

As they pushed from the vehicle, moving towards the bar, she realized perhaps the same could be said for this establishment.

The vehicles outside were all expensive cars. She didn't recognize most of them, but half looked like spaceships. Blue and red with spoilers and occasional racing stripes. Other vehicles were more luxurious, stately automobiles.

Forester whistled softly as they passed one of the vehicles.

The moment they stepped inside, the pungent smell of stale beer and cigarettes assaulted their senses. The place was packed, with every seat at the bar taken and groups of people clustered around tables playing pool or darts. Artemis scanned the room, searching for anyone who looked like they worked at the establishment.

Artemis couldn't help but feel out of place as they moved into the dimly lit bar. The music was loud and pulsing, bodies swaying and bumping against each other on the dance floor. She caught the eye of the bouncer at the door, his gaze lingering on her a beat too long before he nodded them in.

As they made their way to the bar, Artemis couldn't help but notice the way the men were looking at her. It wasn't the first time she'd been in such a situation, but it still made her skin crawl. She could feel the tension rising in her body, a knot forming in her stomach.

Forester ordered them both a drink, and they leaned against the bar, scanning the room. Artemis could feel the heat of someone's gaze on her back, and she turned to see a man watching her from across the room. He was tall and muscular, his gaze predatory. There was a flicker of anger in his eyes as he stared at her, and she inched closer to Forester.

She looked away, feeling a shiver run down her spine. She didn't want to be here. She didn't want to deal with any of this. But she had to find out what happened to Marcy, and this was the only lead they had.

The bartender glanced over at them as Forester raised a hand.

Artemis was watching the patrons. The hole-in-the-wall establishment didn't look like much.

But the clientele matched their cars. The expensive jewelry on wrists or in ears, the designer shoes and outfits, all drew the eye.

The faces of the patrons glowed with confidence and hunger. They exuded an air of entitlement in the way they walked, laughed a bit too loudly, danced a bit too aggressively, as if they were used to getting what they wanted. Artemis couldn't help but wonder if Marcy had belonged to this world.

As she scanned the room, her eyes landed on a woman sitting alone at a table in the corner. Unlike the rest of the clientele, she was dressed simply in jeans and a t-shirt. Artemis couldn't help but feel drawn to her.

"Hey," she nudged Forester and gestured towards the woman. "Let's go talk to her."

Forester gave her a quizzical look but followed her lead as they made their way over to the table.

"Mind if we join you?" Artemis asked, trying to sound friendly.

The woman looked up at them, her eyes wary. "Depends on what you want."

Artemis could see the tension in the woman's shoulders, as if she was ready to bolt at any moment. "We're just trying to find out some information about someone. Marcy Thomas. Did you know her?"

The woman's expression softened slightly. She had plain features but kind eyes. She was glancing around the room and playing with car keys. Perhaps she'd been enlisted as the designated driver, though, she did seem out of place... There was something strange about this woman, but Artemis couldn't quite put her finger on what. Not just the mannerisms, the outfit, the calm... Something else.

But Artemis' mind was still whirring.

"What was the name again?"

"Marcy Thomas." Artemis showed a picture on her phone.

The plain-faced woman leaned in, blinked, then nodded once. Her intelligent eyes flashing.

"Yeah, I knew her. She used to come in here sometimes."

Artemis leaned in closer. "What can you tell us about her?"

The woman hesitated before speaking. "I don't know much... who's asking?"

Forester flashed his badge, and the woman suddenly tensed. She swallowed briefly, shrugged, then said, "Feds? Is this about the murders?"

"Yeah," Forester said simply.

"Oh, God. Okay... Umm... I didn't know her well. Not at all! But I do know she was seeing someone. A guy who came in here sometimes. He was... intense. Always had a lot of money and flashy cars. I heard they had a big fight one night."

"A fight?" Artemis said.

"Yeah. Screaming in the bathroom. Threats. This whole thing. I wasn't there, but I heard about it from some of the others around here." She nodded towards a man with spiky blonde hair behind the bar.

Artemis glanced over then turned back to look at the woman sitting at the table. "What are you doing here?" she said slowly.

"How do you mean?" The woman had to lean forward to be heard over the pulsing music.

"I mean," Artemis said quietly, "You look out of place."

The woman blinked, a knowing look in her eyes. Then she gave a faint smile, shaking her head. She said, quickly, "I've actually got to go. Good chatting."

She pushed to her feet, and before Artemis could protest, slipped off onto the dance floor, moving between the writhing bodies.

Artemis watched the woman go then shook her head, frowning.

She turned and shared a look with Forester. He glanced towards the bartender. Then his eyes moved, tracing back towards the young woman moving away from them.

He frowned suddenly and nudged Artemis.

The two of them peered through the dingy bar, across the dance floor, towards where the woman with the intelligent eyes had paused and was speaking with a couple of young men boasting spiky hair and silver chains.

The young men were arguing with her about something, but the woman didn't budge, shaking her head a single time.

Finally, the men, grumbling, extended something to her.

She slipped something into one of their pockets and then moved on, hurrying away.

Artemis and Forester both stared.

"Was that what I think it was?" Forester said slowly.

"A drug deal?" Artemis replied, tense.

The plain-faced woman glanced back at them, flashing a quick, mischievous grin, and then she hastened out the back door, under a glowing red EXIT sign.

Forester and Artemis both cursed, moving in tandem, trying to hasten in hot pursuit of the drug dealer.

They burst out into the cool night air, scanning the dimly lit alleyway for any sign of the woman. The alley was empty, save for a few overflowing trash cans and a couple of rats scurrying away from the sudden noise.

"Where the hell did she go?" Forester muttered, frustration clear in his voice.

Artemis shook her head, then pointed towards a small door at the end of the alleyway. "There," she said firmly, already moving towards it.

Forester followed, his hand reaching for the gun at his waist.

The door was unlocked, and they burst through it, scanning the dimly lit room beyond. It was a small storage room, filled with boxes and crates stacked haphazardly.

"Clear," Forester muttered as Artemis moved towards a door on the other side of the room.

It led to a narrow staircase, and at the top, they emerged onto a rooftop, the city skyline looming in the distance.

Artemis heard the clang of footsteps against metal.

"Fire escape!" she called, pointing towards a back rail.

The two of them bolted towards it.

They stared down as the young woman slipped out the base of the fire escape and moved hastily towards a sleek, red convertible. A Corvette Stingray by the look of it.

The woman was moving fast now.

The car's lights flickered as the doors unlocked, and she slipped into the front seat.

Forester and Artemis both pursued down the metal fire escape steps.

The Corvette was revving its engine now, and tires squealed against the ground as the vehicle began to speed away.

"Car!" Artemis yelled. "Cameron!"

The keys were already in his hand, jangling as he took long loping steps ahead of her, back out of the alley, sprinting towards where they'd left their vehicle.

Artemis chased behind him, staring after the fleeing Corvette as if certain it might vanish should she look away.

Cameron was quick to start their car and pull out onto the street, Artemis hopping into the passenger seat. They sped down the dark, deserted road, following the red blur of the Corvette in front of them.

"Can you get a plate number?" Cameron asked, his eyes fixed on the road ahead.

Artemis pulled out her phone, trying to steady her hands as she zoomed in and snapped a picture of the license plate.

"Got it," she said, showing the screen to Cameron.

He nodded, his jaw clenched in determination. "Call it in. See if they have—"

"No need," Artemis replied quickly.

"What?"

He shot her a look.

"It's Julius Bateman's car," she replied.

"The dead billionaire?"

"Yeah. I saw the car parked in his driveway."

"What's a drug dealer doing in a murder victim's Corvette?"

They followed the sports car rapidly, the chase weaving through the dusty roads, the speeding cars swerving through intersections.

Headlights flashed, and Forester leaned on the horn, the sound blaring in the night.

But the car ahead of them refused to slow down.

Artemis pointed up ahead, and Forester nodded, showing he'd seen.

The Corvette pulled into a gated driveway, the high brick walls surrounding the estate looming ominously in the darkness.

The gated area wasn't *quite* as nice as Mr. Bateman's billionaire paradise had been.

But the view was better.

Off to their left, Artemis spotted a clearing in the trees, and in the distance, her eyes found a meandering coastline, teased by rolling waves.

The water sat as an expanse on the horizon, reminding Artemis of just how small she really was.

But now, the figure in the Corvette had emerged from her vehicle and was racing up the steps into a large mansion.

Forester and Artemis both reached the gate.

But the bright, metal blockade didn't part for them as it had for her.

A man was sitting in a guard booth, eyeing them both suspiciously. Artemis and Forester exchanged a look, then Forester stepped out of the car and approached the guard booth.

"Federal agents," he said, holding up his badge.

The guard scrutinized it, then leaned forward, clicking his fingers.

Forester extended the badge, and the guard took his time about studying it.

He hesitated, shook his head, hesitated some more.

Forester snapped, "Enough!"

He leaned into the cubicle, through the window, and pushed the button that opened the gate.

The guard protested, but Forester hastened back to the running vehicle and drove it through the open barricade.

Artemis and Forester both breathed a sigh of relief, then sped up the driveway towards the mansion.

As they approached, Artemis couldn't help but stare in awe at the sheer size of the place. It was a sprawling estate, with multiple wings and levels, all of them lit up with external lanterns and other luxurious fixtures.

Forester pulled the car to a stop, and the two of them got out, moving quickly towards the front doors.

They weren't locked, and they pushed them open, stepping into a grand foyer.

The woman they'd been chasing was nowhere to be seen, but there were voices coming from further inside the mansion.

Artemis and Forester exchanged a look, then moved towards the sound.

They found themselves in a large living room, filled with plush furniture and expensive decor.

There were two men standing in the center of the room, one of them holding a gun.

The woman they'd been chasing was standing off to the side, looking uneasy.

"Federal agents," Forester said, holding up his badge once again.

He had his weapon raised, pointing it at the two men.

But then he froze.

Artemis did as well.

The men were both wearing police uniforms. Both had been speaking in hushed voices with the young woman, but at the sight of Forester's badge and gun, they'd gone quiet.

Now, they had turned to face him.

Neither of the men looked at all perturbed by the gun. There was something steely cold in their eyes.

The scars along one of the men's faces were enough to suggest to Artemis that these officers weren't beat cops.

They'd seen their share of danger.

175

They looked as if they could have been brothers. One of them had a buzz cut, while the other had long hair pulled back into a ponytail.

"Federal agents, huh?" the one with the buzz cut said, his voice dripping with skepticism. "What brings you to our little party?"

Forester didn't answer right away. Artemis could feel the tension in the air, could sense the danger.

"We're investigating the murder of Julius Bateman," Forester finally said. "And your friend here," he nodded to the woman, "was driving the dead man's Corvette."

The two men exchanged a look.

"Never heard of Bateman," the one with the ponytail said.

Artemis looked at the young woman, who was biting her lip nervously.

"You *were* driving his car," she said, her voice barely above a whisper.

The two men's eyes flicked back to her and then to Forester.

"Listen," the one with the buzz cut said. "We don't want any trouble, and we don't know anything about any murder. We're just here to keep the peace. Abigail here is our CI. She called us in and said a couple of goons were following her."

The woman winced sheepishly at this characterization but still lingered back, sticking to the shadows, keeping her distance from Cameron and Artemis.

"We're going to need to see some identification," Forester said, his voice firm. "You two really cops?"

The men hesitated, and Artemis could see the tension building in their bodies. But then, the one with the buzz cut shrugged, his hand still on his own weapon, but his other reaching for his pocket.

"Sure thing," he said, pulling out a wallet and flipping it open to reveal a badge. "Detective Jameson, SPD."

The other man followed suit, revealing his own badge. "Detective Michaels, also SPD."

Forester hesitated a moment, but as Artemis looked the men up and down, she found that she believed them. These were cops. Abigail was their CI.

"CI for what?" she said, frowning.

The two men glanced at her. Abigail didn't though. The young woman was peering out a nearby window, staring out at the coastline in the distance.

Artemis frowned over her shoulder now. The long hallways seemed especially empty all of a sudden. Her attention returned to Abigail.

The two police shared a look, and the one with the buzz cut said, "I'm afraid we're not at liberty to discuss an ongoing investigation."

Forester stepped in now, scowling. "Hang on just one moment," he snapped. "She is driving a murder victim's car. We spotted her dealing drugs at a night club where *another* victim was found who later overdosed on a fentanyl cocktail..." He allowed the words to linger briefly, arching his eyebrows. He concluded with, "And you're now trying to pull *rank*?"

The police officers both tensed. One of them glanced towards where Abigail was still refusing to meet anyone's gaze.

"You were dealing again?" the cop with the pony-tail muttered.

She didn't meet his eyes but shrugged, and said, in a murmur, "You wanted me to get more info. So that's what I was doing."

"Drop it, Jameson," said the one cop.

But Officer Jameson was scowling at Abigail now, shaking his head. "What the hell? Six months of work, and you're trying to piss it away? For what?"

She rounded on him now, glaring, her eyes flashing. Standing by the window, outlined against the scenic background, she looked momentarily like some avenging shade.

A look of such anger crossed her features that it nearly took Artemis' breath away.

"Did you want more info or not?" she snapped.

"Drop it," snarled the first cop.

But now Abigail was shaking her head. "No! You know what, *hell* no!" she said.

"You keep putting my ass in the fire, and you want me to pretend like I'm snorkeling."

The cop blinked. "W-what?"

She shook her head, too angry to slow down and explain the perplexing metaphor. She said, "I got what you wanted. I told you who's been dealing that shit. So I passed off a couple of blunts, big deal!" she yelled. "I've gotta make some cash too."

"And the Corvette?" snapped Jameson. "You took it from the impound lot. Didn't you? I was wondering where the hell you got to at the precinct. Bathroom break my ass."

The two of them were both scowling at each other, arms crossed.

The cop with the pony-tail was sighing, massaging the bridge of his nose and looking weary, as if he were more than used to this sort of interaction between these two.

Artemis glanced back and forth then cleared her throat, stepping forward, her hands half held out as if in surrender.

She said, "We're not trying to edge in on your case. But maybe we can help each other. Correct me if I'm wrong, but those people back at that bar looked like a pretty exclusive bunch."

Abigail nodded fiercely. "Exactly. I needed the car. If I showed up in my damn Toyota, I would've been spotted a mile away."

"Bullshit," snapped officer Jameson. "You were dealing there before."

"When I worked there! Yeah. But getting arrested is a bit of a kick in the teeth, don't you think?" She turned quickly to Artemis and Forester, shaking her head fiercely. "I didn't know that Corvette was a dead guy's car. It was just the nicest one on the lot."

"The impound lot?" Forester said. It wasn't in a disapproving tone, though, but rather as if he were impressed.

"Yeah, well... you know how it is. Almost five hundred horsepower," she said with a smirk.

"I like your style," Forester shot back.

She nodded as if appreciating this compliment but then hurriedly added, "And I'm telling you, I had nothing to do with anyone's murder. You said this was about Marcy Thomas."

"It is," said Artemis.

"Who's Marcy Thomas?" Officer Jameson cut in, scratching at the stubble along his chin.

"Murder victim," said Forester. "Overdosed on a fentanyl cocktail and then was stabbed three times."

Artemis watched Abigail's expression as Forester said this with some interest.

Abigail's eyes widened, and she let out a shuddering little breath of air. She looked sick for a moment and glanced out the window once more.

Was she acting?

It was a believable charade if she was.

Artemis decided to give her the benefit of the doubt for now.

"We think there might be a connection between Marcy's murder and the drugs being dealt at that club," she said.

Abigail nodded slowly, her eyes flicking back and forth between the two officers.

They both looked uneasy again.

Officer Jameson stepped forward, arms crossed, suddenly standing between Artemis and Abigail as if he were a bouncer at a club.

He frowned at her, standing nearly six-foot. Compared to Forester, though, he was a few inches shorter.

Cameron stepped forward as well now, facing the cop.

Guns were pointed at the ground for the moment, but Artemis could feel the tension building.

"I told you," said Abigail quickly, "I didn't know Marcy well. And I didn't know her boyfriend. I just know he was some asshole. That's it."

"You said they fought."

"Yeah, but I didn't hear it. I wasn't there."

Here, though, Jameson paused, clearing his throat. He tensed, glanced at his partner, then back at them.

"What is it?" Artemis said, reading his body language.

He hesitated. "Nothing," he said at last.

But Artemis was now reading him. Taking in the visual cues of his hunched posture, the way his arms had tensed, his fingers clasping against his biceps where they were crossed over one another.

Contrary to popular belief, clenched fists were often a defensive tell. It was the concealing of the vulnerable palm by the fingers.

The crossed arms was a similar position.

Now, though, she spotted a thin layer of sweat along his forehead. The twist of his foot against the ground, squeaking there.

Artemis glanced between the two, and her eyes flickered to Abigail, and then she said, "You're lying to me."

They all stared at her.

She nodded more adamantly now. "All of it... you're lying." She looked at Abigail. "You're not a CI. You're a cop. Undercover."

Everyone had gone still.

Forester tensed at her side. The two officers looked uncomfortable now. Jameson shot a quick glance towards Abigail, but she gave the faintest shake of her head.

"No," Artemis said quickly, reading the accusatory glance, "She didn't tell me. But you're investigating the murders too. Aren't you? You also think it's tied to the drugs."

The two cops were both staring directly at her. Abigail was now also gaping in Artemis' direction.

Artemis just nodded more adamantly, her conviction rising. She was fishing, but the looks on their faces confirmed it.

"That's why you lied to us, isn't it? You are investigating me. That's why. You set up, waiting for me to arrive at the bar. Someone tipped you off." She paused and then said, "Forester, our car is bugged."

Jameson's eyes flickered, and then in an outburst, he rounded on Abigail and snapped, "What the hell have you been saying?"

But Abigail just shook her head. "I didn't say anything."

Forester was glaring at everyone now, but then, suddenly, he let out a whooshing little breath. "Shit. You're Deputy Director Schmidt, aren't you? You didn't bug the car, you tapped our phones."

Now, the woman who'd been called Abigail seemed to consider them both. Finally, she shrugged once and seemed to briefly relax.

She let out a long breath and stepped forward.

Everything about her posture, her attitude seemed to shift.

She brushed her hair out of her eyes, and she glanced between the two of them with some interest. Artemis had the distinct feeling that she was being examined by a shark in open waters.

CHAPTER 20

"YOU REALLY ARE AS clever as your file says," said Abigail. "Aren't you?"

Artemis felt a cold chill along her back. Abigail extended her hand. "Harmony Schmidt. It's good to finally meet you in person."

Artemis could feel her pulse quickening. Had her phone really been tapped? Had someone been listening in on her conversations? They'd done their best to keep their voices disguised and conversations short with her brother and father.

But what had this woman heard?

She'd known enough to set up shop at the bar, *Biggie's Small.*

The plain-faced woman with the intelligent eyes and regal posture didn't blink now.

She said, "What are you doing here, Artemis Blythe?"

The two officers both looked confused now.

Forester looked as if he wasn't sure if he ought to punch the problem at hand.

But Artemis could only feel her stomach twisting in knots as she tried to comprehend what was going on.

It was like watching a transformation occur in Abigail. In a way, prompted by a thought that brought chills, Artemis was reminded of her father's own transformations.

Deputy Director Harmony Schmidt.

Forester had warned her that someone was looking into their team. Someone who had it out for Supervising Agent Grant.

Someone who'd been assigned to bring down Forester, Wade, and Artemis.

But the big bad boogeyman didn't look so scary up close.

The woman who'd been playing Artemis from the start, who'd likely overheard where they were headed and set up shop back at the bar, was standing there, her expression amused and quizzical.

"I... so all of this talk about drugs," Artemis said slowly. "You were just yanking our chains?"

Officer Jameson began to reply, and judging by the inclination of his nose, it was going to be a snide remark.

Before he could speak, though, Harmony stepped forward, putting a hand on his arm and pressing him back.

He moved without protest.

She said, quietly, "I'm afraid not. These kind officers here were nice enough to allow me to tag along with their taskforce. But I'm afraid the drugs are very real, and... the murders have caught our attention."

"I... I don't understand..." Artemis said.

She felt a faint shiver up her spine. She had the sudden and distinct impression that she was no longer the one interviewing Abigail. But rather, she was now the one due for an interrogation.

Instead of answering Artemis' confusion, the woman said, "Is it true that your brother still has connections with the Seattle Mob?"

Artemis blinked.

Forester had gone still at her side.

"I... I mean, yes. But I don't see what that has to do with—"

"And is it also true that you were in contact with Julius Bateman right before he died?"

Suddenly, Artemis' eyebrows shot up. She stammered, then began to shake her head hurriedly. "Hang on just one moment!"

"And," Harmony interrupted, raising a manicured fingernail, "It's also true that you have experience with pharmaceutical procedures, no? Your own sister, when she was young, was on some very heavy medications. Did it familiarize you with narcotics? Is that why you're here, Artemis Blythe?"

Now, the whole confusing situation made sense.

It all settled on Artemis like a load of bricks, weighing her down.

She was under investigation.

Not only that, but these two officers had been so convinced she was a suspect, they'd been willing to go along with the ruse in order to try and capture her.

The looks of confusion had been real when Artemis had started questioning them. And Officer Jameson had panicked when he'd thought that Harmony had spilled the beans.

The emotions made sense, but the way in which she'd interpreted them was now wildly different.

"You know, I play chess myself sometimes," said the deputy director. She nodded. "Nowhere near as well as you do. But I've studied your games, Ms. Blythe. All of them, in fact. You do seem to have a penchant for opening queen side but sacrificing material for position."

If there was some veiled inference in this comment, Artemis didn't spot it.

She was still too busy reeling, her mind racing at this revelation.

Now, seeing Harmony Schmidt in a new light, Artemis spotted more details about the woman. The plain clothing seemed to suit her. But her hair had been brushed in such a way as to hide a shaved portion on the right side of her face.

The way she stood, the way she moved, Artemis guessed this was a *very* athletic woman. Her muscle tone was impressive, even with the simple t-shirt and slacks.

She had a hemp bracelet visible around one wrist, twisted with a few strands of vibrant color.

Her eyes were piercing, attentive. And the intelligence that Artemis had initially noted was off-putting.

This wasn't just a bright woman. It was an *extremely* bright woman.

And Artemis happened to be in her crosshairs.

"You go to all this trouble for that?" Forester said at last, snorting.

He stood under a chandelier, his feet spread at shoulder width on a luxurious silk, Turkish carpet. Everything from his hand clenched around his weapon to his jutting chin was a posture of defiance.

"You're wasting valuable time, lady."

But Harmony Schmidt turned to him now. "Cameron Forester," she said softly. "I've heard a lot about you. From your aunt, in fact."

"Yeah? My auntie told me about you," Cameron said. "Nothing nice, I promise."

189

"Well... At least some things never change." There was a note of ice in the woman's voice.

"You're barking up the wrong tree," Forester snapped.

"Are you calling me a bitch?" A smile. "I suppose I am that. In a way. You know, I have an incentive to see you brought to justice. Both of you. Grant too. Wade also. I know all about your little team."

"What incentive?" Artemis said.

"Nothing too romantic. A cash reward." Harmony shrugged simply. There wasn't an ounce of shame or apology in her tone. She simply stated it matter-of-factly like an oncologist with no bedside manner delivering a diagnosis.

Artemis kept glancing over her shoulder, through the large mansion.

Now that she was looking, she realized this place hadn't been lived in in some time. No jackets, dust on the handrails of the stairs, the lights off. Some of the electrical outlets only with wires jutting out. And even the Turkish carpet was stained in portions and burnt towards the back edge, furthest from Artemis, near a now dormant fireplace.

Above, the chandelier was missing glass baubles.

This, evidently, was where Harmony had set up her team in order to keep an eye on Artemis and Forester.

Because she thought they were involved.

She suspected them of murder.

But Artemis had faced such accusations before. This time, she said, "We can account for our whereabouts when we found out about Julius Bateman's death." Even as she said it, Artemis hesitated. She remembered now that they had been breaking into the warehouse before Bateman's body was found.

She grimaced.

But before she could recover, Harmony said, "Oh... I know you didn't *personally* kill him. But your brother has business interests that Mr. Bateman was dabbling in. And you're nothing if not resourceful, Ms. Blythe."

Artemis felt a strange chill at these words, but Forester suddenly interjected. "Got evidence? Hmm? Anything? Cuz if not, we're walking. What a waste of time. Holy shit. They pay you for this bullshit?"

His temper was getting the best of him.

But Harmony just smiled again, running a hand through her hair, and revealing the shaved side of her head.

She shook her head once. "I'm just keeping an eye on things, Ms. Blythe. Mr. Forester."

Cameron just snorted, grabbed Artemis by the arm, and tugged her towards the door insistently. "Let's get out of here. Just wasting our time."

But Artemis was frowning. "All that stuff about seeing Marcy Thomas get into a fight. Was that true?"

"Yes. That was true. I didn't see it, but an informant of ours did." "Do you know who she fought with?"

"Yes. Mr. Bateman," said Schmidt simply. "Who also happens to be the supplier of fentanyl in this area. He ships them here—"

"Inside arrow heads," Artemis said suddenly.

And for the first time, Harmony looked impressed. "Very good," she murmured.

Now it made sense why Julius' name had been on the shipment of arrows. But someone had kidnapped his daughter Kayla. Someone had killed his daughter's friend, Marcy Thomas. Someone had shot Whitney Martin with arrows.

And then someone had murdered Bateman.

Was this all to do with drug dealing?

Was Artemis approaching this from the wrong angle?

"How did you know about Mr. Bateman's methods?" said Schmidt now.

"Artemis, let's go," Forester insisted.

She hesitated. Harmony was still watching her. But Artemis doubted that telling the woman that she'd been breaking and entering and stealing data from a computer would do anything for improving her standing.

So she said nothing.

She began to move back towards the door, following Forester.

At any moment, she half expected Harmony to call after them. For her to place them under arrest.

But the words never came.

Artemis could feel the strange woman's eyes lingering on her, watching as she drew nearer to the door, following with Agent Forester. It was as if Harmony had *wanted* them to know she was there, that she was watching. But for now, she was like a spider who had decided to allow a fly to escape its web.

Artemis shivered as they hastened away.

The two of them pushed out into the night, facing the coast again.

Only once they had closed the door behind them, did Forester say under his breath, "I think I know who's behind all this."

Artemis shot him a quick glance.

He nodded. His eyes distant, pained.

"Really?"

He paused, swallowed, then said, "I think so. Come on—let's move."

CHAPTER 21

AS THEY RACED AWAY from the mansions, along the coast, Forester turned to Artemis.

He had a troubled look in his eyes, and the wind whipping through his open window caused his already tussled hair to dance with the wind.

His eyes were rigid, though, unblinking, carrying something hidden.

"What is it?" Artemis asked softly. "Who's behind this?"

"I... It's revenge."

She frowned, glancing at him. Her own anxiety was still rising. The thought that the FBI was investigating them, had gone out of their way to try and trick them... It made her skin crawl.

Was it normal for a deputy director to go into the field herself?

Not normal at all, Artemis imagined. There was something different about Harmony Schmidt. Something far more *hands-on*.

And it made her skin crawl. She'd have to be infinitely more careful now. She'd been hoping to return home and visit her sister after this case.

But now everything was collapsing around them.

The reward had died with Julius Bateman. His daughter was still missing, though.

And Artemis still didn't know who was behind all of this.

She shoved aside thoughts of Harmony, of the FBI. She still had her damn field tests to pass this weekend.

No... No, there was too much to focus on to allow her mind to worry.

But though she could reason with herself, she couldn't alter the twisting knot forming in her stomach.

Still, Forester didn't look too perturbed. Instead, he was saying, "It's the only thing that makes sense to me. He didn't fit the pattern."

"Who didn't? Julius?"

"Exactly. The other three victims were young women. The first one overdosed and then was stabbed. The second was shot with arrows. And the third barely survived."

"There are so many people involved, though," Artemis said.

"Yeah. Yeah... I know..." He frowned, trailing off. "But it's revenge."

"You're sure?"

"Yeah. Look what they did to him."

Artemis just glanced at her partner. She supposed if anyone would know the flavors of vengeance, it would be Forester.

Still, her stomach was continuing to twist and turn. Her heartbeat resounded in her chest.

"Why are you so calm?" she suddenly blurted out.

For a brief moment, it was as if she wasn't even listening to the conversation. As if thoughts of the sordid murders, the bleeding billionaires, and all their problems had been temporarily forgotten.

Forester just glanced at her, frowning. "Calm?"

"Yeah! You just heard we're being investigated. Why are you so calm?"

"I already knew that."

"Yeah, but... but..." She stared at him.

He looked back at her quizzically.

Sometimes she forgot that Forester wasn't mentally typical. Anti-social personality disorder could affect the broad range of human emotions sometimes.

One emotion, though, it often seemed to affect in Cameron was fear.

He didn't have the same anxieties or nerves that Artemis so often struggled with.

She often felt as if she were knocked about by winds and waves, whereas he was a granite pillar, unaffected by any of it.

Forester just shrugged, waving a hand casually as they whipped along the coast. "Been investigated before," he said. "Not news. Just history. She can't take Grant."

"Excuse me?"

"Harmony," he said. "She's good. But she's not Grant. Don't worry about it."

"I am worried."

"I can see that. Don't."

"I can't just turn it off, Cameron."

He shrugged. "Well, I'm telling you... People have come at Grant before. It'll be fine."

Artemis watched him, her eyes narrowed. She wondered if he was just saying this to comfort her. Or if he really believed it.

With her, Forester often seemed to tell the truth.

It was one of the things she liked about him.

Now, though, he was saying, "Look, don't let her distract you. I'm telling you, this was vengeance. They took him out for revenge."

"Who?"

"Someone who wanted Julius Bateman dead," he replied. "And someone who wanted those others dead too."

Artemis frowned now. "What makes you so sure?"

"He didn't fit the pattern. The way they killed him was personal."

"So... if he was shipping fentanyl into the area," Artemis said quietly. "Then... then..."

They continued to drive along the coast, and Forester kept to five miles below the speed limit, going at his own pace like usual.

The tree-lined coast lined by state parks and two-lane roads seemed like the border of some painting, outlined in gray asphalt. The waves moved in a mesmerizing pattern, rolling against the shore in a slow and steady rhythm. Artemis could feel herself getting lost in the scenery, the sound of the waves, the smell of the ocean.

But Forester's words brought her back to reality.

"It's possible," he said, his eyes still fixed on the road. "But I don't think it's just the fentanyl. Something doesn't add up. He wasn't just a drug dealer. He had connections, money... Maybe it was a power struggle. Maybe someone wanted him out of the picture."

Artemis nodded slowly, her mind racing with possibilities. She knew Forester was right. There was something more to this case than just drug trafficking. There were too many unanswered questions. They had five men in custody who'd been willing to *kill*. Money was behind all of this mess. The five men were being defended by expensive lawyers, all of them tight-lipped, refusing to speak.

As they drove on, though, Artemis couldn't help but think about the danger they were in. The FBI was watching them, and they had no idea who was behind the murders.

But she also couldn't shake off the feeling that they were getting closer to the truth. That they were on the brink of solving this case.

She glanced over at Forester, who was still staring ahead, his expression unreadable.

As they drove on, the knot in her stomach began to unravel, replaced by a newfound determination. This was the missing piece.

Vengeance.

"She overdosed," Artemis said quietly. "Marcy Thomas overdosed and was *then* stabbed."

Forester glanced at her. "What are you saying?"

"What if she wasn't a murder victim? What if you're right. What if all of this comes back to vengeance?"

Forester blinked, staring at her. "Come again?"

Artemis was nodding now, her head bobbing up and down, her confidence growing. She could feel her excitement rising as the words flowed, "We know she died from an overdose and was then stabbed."

"Yeah? So?"

"So," Artemis said quickly, "What if she died and someone found her. Someone close to her? And what if that someone then decided to disguise *future* murders. No, hang on, let me explain. I know it sounds crazy, but these people..." Artemis was nodding quickly, her own excitement rising. "What if someone found her dead. Maybe her father. A brother. Someone. They found Marcy dead, overdosed, and immediately their thoughts go to vengeance. What if they knew who was dealing fentanyl? They knew Julius was bringing it into the area."

"What about the other girls, though? What about Whitney Martin?"

Artemis suddenly snapped her fingers. "Her family is new to the area. Remember?"

"Yeah, so?"

"What if the Martins moved here because they're involved with the drug trade? What if this is vengeance on the daughters of those who someone blames for Marcy's death?"

Forester was frowning. The water along the coast almost seemed more agitated now, white peaks rising over the infinite gray. Artemis' mismatched eyes peered out the window, narrowed now, her pulse quickening.

It was like solving a chess puzzle, all the pieces available, all the information now spread out in front of her.

It was just down to her intelligence. Down to her willingness to focus on the task.

And now, Forester had provided the linchpin.

Even Harmony had helped. She'd made it clear... Julius Bateman was the one bringing in the fentanyl cocktail.

His daughter Kayla was still missing.

Marcy Thomas overdosed and was only stabbed afterwards.

Why?

"It's all camouflage," Artemis said hurriedly. "I'd bet anything. Whoever found Marcy's body wanted to hide what had happened to her. Or... or wanted to set themselves up for future murders."

"So you mean they found her and then decided to kill these other girls? So Marcy's death wasn't murder?"

"No. No, what if she died by accident. And then someone, someone with a twisted mind, decided to use the arrows. The items Julius and his team were bringing the drugs in with... What if they used the arrows to hunt down the daughters of the men they blamed for Marcy's death? And they stabbed Marcy in order to remove suspicion from themselves."

"Genius," Forester said suddenly. "If Marcy was a victim too, no one would suspect them of being involved. But..." He paused. "Wouldn't it take a lot to... you know, stab your daughter's corpse?"

"Maybe. But maybe whoever did this had one of their armed goons do it. Maybe they saw the vengeance worth the cost." Artemis shrugged. "But I think you're right. I think this is all down to vengeance."

Forester's hands gripped the steering wheel, he was nodding as she spoke. "It makes sense," he said. "Marcy Thomas' family comes from money, anyway."

Artemis shivered. "And who would leave fifty million on the table. The check in Julius' hand. Who would reject it?"

"Someone who was already filthy rich."

"Exactly! We need to get Marcy's family together. Her parents, brothers. Anyone in the area. Anyone who might have done this."

"They won't come down to the precinct."

"That's fine. We've been in a couple of mansions already. Another won't hurt."

"I could get used to this lifestyle."

"I doubt it. You can't even button your suit right."

He smirked at her. Then, quick, leaned in and stole a kiss.

She found herself smiling when he looked away and settled in her seat.

But just as quickly, her smile vanished.

Kayla Bateman was still out there. Someone had tried to kill Whitney Martin in the hospital. Someone had already murdered a girl and Julius.

They had to hurry.

Lives were on the line, and the bleakest part of night was coming quickly.

CHAPTER 22

KAYLA SHIVERED, LISTENING TO the dim echoes of water dripping around her.

She stared through the gaps in the moldered floorboards at her feet, watching as two figures moved out of sight.

A man and a woman. The woman had bright, flowing red hair. They both wore golden masks.

They were holding a whispered conversation.

And she caught words like, "...too late. Hospital was overrun."

"We still could've done it," the woman replied.

"No. Not that way. There's still time. Trust me."

Then they disappeared from sight, leaving Kayla alone with her thoughts, trembling and shivering.

She closed her eyes.

After her second escape attempt, they'd moved her once more.

She'd felt certain, when they'd come for her, that she was going to die.

But then the phone calls had come in.

The red-haired woman had hastened away. Kayla had been left un-harmed.

For now.

They'd taken her to this new room, a hood over her head which she'd only just managed to remove.

Her hands were chained. Her legs bound.

She sat in an old, worn room. The walls were charred, ashen. The floorboards splintered.

She thought she recognized the place as a burnt mansion on a bluff overlooking the coast—when she'd been younger, some of her friends had dared her to explore the place at night.

Now, the fears she'd imagined as a child had become all too real as an adult.

She shivered again, trying to stay quiet. Trying to pretend as if she wasn't moving.

The camera over the door was directed at her. Watching her.

But her fingers were nearly slipped through the shackle.

The cuffs that had been used had been sloppily applied, and she'd flexed her wrists when they'd done it.

Now, the wiggle room she'd given herself allowed her hands to slowly slip free.

It was a painful experience, pulling her hands from the metal, and especially painful as she had to do it surreptitiously, to avoid being spotted by the camera.

But now, with a pained gasp, her left hand popped free.

She kept it raised, head low, still pretending as if nothing had changed.

But a flare of elation filled her.

This time...

She had to escape.

They'd promised to torture her to death if she didn't. Why were they still keeping her alive?

What did they want?

Kayla shivered, her heart pounding. She summoned her nerve. The moment they spotted her hands were free, trouble would come. But she had to hurry.

She couldn't stay here. Who knew when they'd come back for her?

She summoned her resolve, rehearsing what she intended to do in her mind.

She could hear the guard outside her door breathing heavily. He was watching her on his phone, keeping an eye on the security footage.

She had to move faster than he did.

Faster than he spotted her escape.

"Come on," she whispered to herself.

And then Kayla moved fast.

She slipped the second hand through the cuffs now.

There was no time to spare. Everything had to go quickly. She had to move through the rehearsed choices.

Hands free, she pulled at the sharp end of the cuff, rubbing it rapidly against the ropes around her ankles.

Small fibers of rope began to fall away, and she worked feverishly, ignoring the pain in her wrists and ankles.

Judging by the shadow under the door, the guard outside her door still hadn't noticed the developments with the security footage. She took a deep breath, ignoring the shivers still wracking her body. The ropes finally came away. Tumbling on the ground.

Then she rose, slowly, silently, and crept towards the far window.

Her heart pounding, she took a step forward, then another.

She was almost at the door when a sudden beep emanated from behind her. A notification sound. A buzzer?

A phone, she realized.

She went still, panicked.

And then came a shout.

The door was flung open, and a man lunged into the room, gun in hand.

He looked up, startled, and their eyes met. For a moment, they froze, staring at each other.

And then Kayla reacted. She flung herself through the window.

The glass shattering around her. A gunshot resounding from the room, the bullet barely missing.

And she fell, plummeting with shards of glass in a desperate bid for freedom.

This time, if she was caught, she was dead.

CHAPTER 23

THEY MARCHED UP THE impressive, carved wood steps to the mansion. The whole thing looked like an ornate log cabin, with multiple levels and naked, treated wood. The beam post entrance sheltered a redwood door with intricate carvings along the frame.

Artemis wasn't sure she'd seen a mansion made of logs before, but the small waterfall trickling *under* an elevated, glass walkway between two wings of the house attracted her eye immediately.

She couldn't help but admire the craftsmanship, but her mind was focused on the task at hand. They had to find out who was behind the murders and stop them before anyone else got hurt.

Forester rang the doorbell, and they waited in tense silence. The door opened, and a young man in a suit greeted them. "Can I help you?"

Artemis stepped forward. "We're here to speak with the Thomas family. It's regarding their daughter, Marcy."

The young man's expression turned cold. He had handsome features, but his ears stuck out a bit too far. His dark hair was combed to the side like a choir boy's, but he had to have been in his twenties. "I'm sorry, but the family is not receiving visitors at this time."

"We're with the police," Forester interjected. "We called ahead. It's important that we speak with them."

The young man hesitated, looking them up and down skeptically. "Mind if I see some ID?"

Forester flashed his badge.

The man sighed. "Very well. Follow me."

He led them through the spacious mansion, past paintings and sculptures worth more than most people's houses. They arrived at a large study, and the young man gestured for them to wait.

The study was impressive, with mahogany bookcases lining the walls and a fireplace crackling with warmth.

Artemis and Forester stood on a smooth, varnished floor, both waiting near the fireplace.

They glanced towards a door at the far end of the room from where they could both hear the tapping sound of approaching footsteps.

Artemis could feel her nerves rising again.

She wasn't sure what she'd expected... But they'd called ahead. They'd asked for the Thomas family to gather.

Now...

Now, in the empty study, she was wondering if they'd just voluntarily strode into a lion's den.

The young man had disappeared.

And the tapping footsteps drew closer.

A few moments later, a middle-aged man entered the room. He was tall and thin, with greying hair and a stern expression on gaunt features. He didn't start with pleasantries. Didn't introduce himself or greet them. His gaze swept over them a single time as if this one glance gave him all the information he needed about them.

This, his voice resounding, he said, "What is this about?"

Artemis took a deep breath.

But Forester cut in. "Are you Arthur Thomas?"

"That's right."

"You're Marcy's father."

"Is that what this is about?" he snapped. "At this hour?"

"I'm afraid so. We need to speak with the rest of your family. Like I said on the phone, it's not a request. Either we speak here or downtown."

Mr. Thomas' eyes narrowed. He clearly wasn't a man accustomed to being told what to do.

Artemis could feel her own anxiety threatening to overtake her. Her eyes darted to the fire then back to the billionaire.

"Now, please. Who else is here?" Forester said. "We need to speak with all the suspects."

Mr. Thomas's eyes widened in shock. "What are you saying? *Suspects*?"

Forester had intentionally inserted the word. Artemis and Cameron knew the best way to keep Thomas off guard was to make him nervous.

Now, some of his angry veneer faded, along with the redness in his face.

Pale, eyes wide, he stammered a couple of times, then turned. "I'll... I'll be right..." he trailed off, frowning.

Then he hastened away once again, back through the door.

This time, the tapping footsteps moved with far more urgency.

It didn't take long, however, for him to return. This time, the footsteps were accompanied by others.

Four figures entered the room.

The handsome man with the jutting ears and choir boy hair came first. Behind him, a young man who looked *identical* to the first, except his hair was spiky with a streak of red dye.

Then came Mr. Thomas and a far younger woman who might have been his daughter, but on closer inspection—aided by the way she kept leaning against him, her hand trailing in his—Artemis decided this was his younger wife.

But she pushed those thoughts aside as the family entered the room. Mr. and Mrs. Thomas sat side by side on a loveseat while their two sons sat across from them in armchairs.

Once everyone had settled, all eyes fixated on Forester and Artemis, a quiet silence fell.

The only sound was the crackle of the fire. And, in Artemis' case, the pounding of her heart.

Four sets of eyes stared at her.

Were these the eyes of murderers?

Artemis leaned forward, her eyes scanning each of their faces. "I know this is a difficult time for all of you," she began, and her voice felt frail and weak, but her mind was agile, studying them, taking in every detail she could, "but we need to ask you a few questions about Marcy's death."

Mr. Thomas cleared his throat. "We've already spoken to the police about this. We have nothing more to say."

But Artemis spoke up. The direct approach, she decided, wouldn't work. This was a man used to being in control. Used to getting his way.

But something stood out to her.

He hadn't lawyered up.

Why?

Why did a man with infinite resources agree to speak with them directly? Why had he brought his family along without legal counsel?

Because he wanted to present himself as innocent? Or because he really was?

This troubled her.

Had she been wrong?

It was far too early to tell.

She kept her tone neutral, kind as she said, "I understand that this is a difficult time for you, but we just want to make sure that we have all the facts straight. Can you tell us what you remember about the night Marcy died?"

Mrs. Thomas shifted in her seat and looked down at her lap. She sniffed.

The woman had cascading red hair which framed her face. She was strikingly beautiful, which only made the apparent age difference between her and her husband all the more obvious.

Forester, clearly noting the same discrepancy, cut in and said, "Excuse me, but how old are you?"

The woman blinked.

The twins, her sons, both shared uncomfortable glances. Mr. Thomas had a steely look in his eyes.

"I... pardon me?"

"How old are you?" he said again, clearly indifferent to social norms. "Marcy was in her twenties, wasn't she?"

"Twenty-four," Artemis said, remembering what Mr. Bateman had told them. She paused now, her brow flickering. A few years older than Kayla. Twenty-four. Well-liked...

She drew on the memory of the exchange with Julius Bateman. It struck her as odd... Why odd?

She frowned.

"I'm turning forty-five," said Mrs. Thomas with a sniff. "I'm only eight years younger than my husband if that's what you're asking. I had Marcy young."

The woman didn't look a day over thirty-two. Artemis wondered exactly how much work had been done to keep her features youthful.

Now, though, as if wanting to move on from the subject of her age, Mrs. Thomas quickly said, "We were all here that night. Watching TV. Marcy said she was going outside to get some fresh air, and we never saw her again."

Artemis noticed the hesitation in Mrs. Thomas' voice, and she shot a glance at her husband as she spoke.

"What about the neighbors? Did anyone see anything suspicious?" Forester asked. Again, following the indirect approach.

The theory still stood. Someone had taken revenge for Marcy's death. Someone had staged it like a murder.

Someone in this room... The only family Marcy had in the area.

Artemis kept watching Mr. Thomas who was still glaring at them.

At Forester's comment, though, the patriarch shook his head. "We live pretty far out of town. Our nearest neighbor is a good mile away. And even then, they keep to themselves."

Artemis felt a twinge of frustration. She decided to ramp up the line of questioning. To be more direct.

So she said, "Can you tell me anything about Marcy's habits? Anything we should know."

Another uncomfortable glance between Mrs. Thomas and her husband. Some unspoken commentary passed between them.

At last, though, Forester interjected. Again, reliable to cut through social norms. He said, "Your daughter was a drug addict."

Mrs. Thomas winced as if this was the comment she'd been dreading.

Her two sons both stared, looking shocked.

Mr. Thomas, though, just stared at his hands, which he'd folded in his lap. He spoke in a quiet voice after a moment, saying, "She struggled with addiction. Yes. She couldn't get her life under control."

"She was doing her best!" Mrs. Thomas said suddenly, glaring at her husband.

He held up his hands in a weary way, as if this were a conversation they'd had in the past and he didn't want to get into it.

But now, Mrs. Thomas seemed to have found somewhere to direct her anger. She was saying, "You never did give her a chance, did you? You thought she was a waste of time. You wanted to kick her out of the house."

"Not now," he said softy. "We can speak on this later."

Artemis took note of the tension between the couple, but she had a job to do. She needed to get to the truth of Marcy's death, and she wasn't going to let this family dynamic get in her way. She decided to take a different approach.

"Mr. Thomas," she said, turning her attention to the patriarch. "Is there anything you're not telling us? Anything that could be helpful in our investigation?"

He looked up at her, his eyes cold and calculating. "What do you mean?" he asked.

"I mean," Artemis said, her voice steady, "that there are some discrepancies in your story. You say that Marcy went outside for fresh air and never came back. But we know that she was found dead in the woods, miles away from here. It doesn't add up."

Mr. Thomas said nothing, but his face had gone pale. Artemis pressed on.

"Did you have any reason to believe that Marcy was in danger? Did she have any enemies, anyone who might want to harm her?"

Again, silence. But Artemis could see the wheels turning in his head.

"I suggest you start telling us the truth," she said firmly. "Because if we find out that you're lying to us, you're going to be in a lot more trouble than you are now."

"What are you saying?" he demanded.

She leaned in now, having baited the hook. "Did you have anything to do with stabbing your daughter?"

His wife gasped.

The two boys just glared at their father. "I knew it!" the one with the jutting ears yelled, lurching to his feet. "You never liked Marcy. You wanted her gone!"

But Mr. Thomas had surged to his feet, throwing out his arms, puffing his chest. In a wounded voice, he yelled, "I didn't kill my step-daughter!"

Forester leaned in. "Then who did?" he asked.

But Artemis just stared.

A miss.

Step-daughter.

Not daughter.

And now, the twins were both glaring at their father.

Step-father.

Mrs. Thomas had her head in her hands as if she couldn't bear the conversation.

But Artemis' mind was racing now.

"He's always hated Marcy!" yelled one of the twins. "He married for our money—he's a greedy bastard!"

"Be quiet, James!" their mother snapped through tears.

Mr. Thomas looked pale now, terrified.

"She wasn't your daughter?" Artemis said hurriedly.

"She was," Mrs. Thomas interjected quickly. "He loved her in his own way."

"No, he didn't, he never did!" cut in the twin, James. His hands balled as he stood next to his brother, their backs to a bookcase.

Mr. Thomas was still pale, but Artemis could see a flush of anger creeping across his face. He looked ready to snap. At last, he said, his voice trembling, "I did what I could. But she was beyond help. She was an addict. That was it."

"She struggled. She wasn't an addict!" yelled Mrs. Thomas.

"No sense living in denial, dear."

"It's not denial," snapped Mrs. Thomas. Her eyes still red-ringed, but with some fire in her voice now. "For instance, you sometimes act like an asshole. But that doesn't mean you are one. Identity matters, dear. Maybe if you'd treated Marcy better, she wouldn't have been murdered!"

"I didn't kill her!" he retorted. "She was shot with arrows. I don't even know how to shoot."

"She overdosed," Artemis cut in quickly.

She dropped the words like cards being flourished onto a poker table, revealing her hand.

All eyes darted to her, staring.

Shock. Surprise.

Then stammering. Mr. Thomas said, "B-but... we were told she was shot."

"Afterwards," Artemis said quietly, staring at him.

She glanced at the twins as well.

But everyone just looked confused, scared, and surprised.

"Why would anyone shoot her after she was dead?" said Mr. Thomas, wrinkling his nose.

Artemis picked at her nails. "We were hoping you might be able to tell us."

"He killed her!" James yelled. "He's a murderer! He'll come for you next, mom!"

Bickering erupted. Angry retorts. Cruel words.

But Artemis was only half listening. Her mind was moving a million miles a minute now.

It didn't add up.

The assumption had been that someone else had killed Marcy and that her father, out of a desire to get revenge, had staged a murder to camouflage his own actions.

But Mr. Thomas didn't seem the type.

He didn't care for his step-daughter. Why would he suddenly fly into a love-fueled vengeance spree for someone he'd written off?

Had he killed her, then, like the twins were saying?

Not likely either.

She'd overdosed. None of them seemed to have known this.

The surprise, the flaring of the nostrils, the clearings of the throats... It all pointed at genuine shock.

"Where's Marcy's father?" Artemis said suddenly. "We asked you to bring everyone in your family here. Where is he?"

A snort. A roll of the eyes. Mr. Thomas was shaking his head. Mrs. Thomas, with her bright red hair, was still trembling, her eyes downcast.

But there was something in those eyes. The briefest of flickers. Something like... fear.

Or... no.

Something colder.

Was the crying an act? Were the tears fake.

So Artemis asked the question again. "Where's Marcy's father?"

"In prison," Mr. Thomas said with a snort, waving a hand. "He was a good-for-nothing, tax-cheating low-life—"

Before he'd finished, though, the well-dressed twin with the choir-boy hair lunged, with a snarl, flinging himself at his step-father and knocking him to the ground.

"Bite him, James!" the other twin called out, cheering him on. "Hit him!"

Mrs. Thomas didn't react. For a moment, when no one was looking, Artemis glimpsed something like a self-satisfied expression in the woman's eyes.

She was *not* what she presented herself as. A grieving mother, yes.

But not frail nor downtrodden. This was a woman who knew how to play on emotions. A manipulator.

In that brief instance, Artemis spotted the face beneath the mask.

But that didn't mean she was a killer.

Did it?

The woman's shoulders were shaking again. She wasn't watching where one of her sons tussled with his step-father. As if she didn't care.

"Break it up!" Forester was yelling, the large FBI agent moving in to intervene. He was stronger than both of the men... combined.

And so it didn't take long for him to separate the two. They were both gasping, their hair disheveled, faces now red and slicked with sweat.

Forester held them apart, scowling, gripping both by their arms. "Cut it out!" he snapped.

Artemis watched as the chaos around her slowly settled. The twins were now sulking in one corner, while Mr. Thomas was nursing his bruises in another. Mrs. Thomas was still crying, but now it seemed to be for show. Forester was pacing, his eyes scanning the room. This was not what they had expected. They had come here to find a killer, but instead, they had found a family that was falling apart.

Artemis couldn't shake the feeling that something was off. She had spent years studying people, trying to understand what made them tick. Something was hidden beneath the surface, something that they weren't seeing.

She cleared her throat and began to speak. But before she could, Forester suddenly cut in.

He was standing between the twins and their step-father, but now he had his phone in his hand and was frowning.

"Kellen Mattheus?" he said suddenly.

Everyone looked up as if they'd been slapped, staring at him.

Forester repeated the name a bit more firmly, raising an eyebrow.

Artemis just watched, confused.

But then, Mr. Thomas said, "That was his name. Why?"

"We all took my husband's name when I left Mattie," said Mrs. Thomas quietly, glancing at Cameron.

The twins looked startled at the mention of their father's name.

"What is it?" Artemis said, turning to Forester.

But before he could reply, she stared at how he gripped his phone. His sudden frown.

She said, softly, "He was released, wasn't he? How long ago."

"He's not due out for another year," said Mr. Thomas.

But Forester was shaking his head. "He was released three months ago for good behavior. Mattheus isn't in prison at all."

Mr. Thomas looked as if he were standing on wobbly legs now. His mouth a circle.

The twins looked stunned.

But Mrs. Thomas didn't look surprised at all. She cleared her throat, excused herself with a mumble, saying something like, "...sorry... restroom."

And then she moved through a side door, hastening away. As she glanced back, her eyes were wide, her face pale.

In fact, something about her expression sent shivers up Artemis' spine.

"So Marcy's father was out of prison when she overdosed?" Artemis said quietly as Mrs. Thomas left.

Forester held her gaze then nodded once.

They paused. A few seconds later, they both heard an odd growling sound. An engine of sorts. A motor?

But the sound faded a second later.

Artemis hesitated, her brow wrinkling.

"We need to find him," Artemis said. "We need to find him right now."

CHAPTER 24

FORESTER MOVED SILENTLY IN the dark, under the cover of midnight, his eyes fixated on the small trailer settled at the foot of the buff.

The scent of salt lingered on the ocean-side air. The sand indented under his footsteps. He glanced back. Artemis had agreed to move around the back of the trailer, as she wasn't armed.

And according to Mattheus' profile, he had been charged in the past with illegally possessing a firearm.

Now, Forester picked up the pace, his eyes fixated on the glow coming from the front window of the trailer.

The trailer was illegally parked, of course. Hidden by the shelter of the trees blocking this portion of the shoreline from view.

As he moved, Forester took a moment to scan the beach, the water. It brought memories back. Memories of the time he'd hunted his wife's killer.

And what he'd done when he'd found the man.

Artemis knew now. She knew and hadn't rejected him.

And she'd told him what she'd done. About her father, her sister.

He had to give her credit. There was far more to Artemis Blythe than met the eye.

And even as the wind picked up, ruffling his hair, bringing a cold chill along his skin, Forester knew he had to be honest with himself.

Things between the two of them had changed.

He paused, fifty feet away from the emanating glow of the trailer's window.

His own shadow still hid in the larger shadows of the bluff.

The coastline itself captured his attention for a moment. Even creeping in the dark, the rocky outcrop set over the choppy water was a beautiful sight to behold, illuminated only by the glow of the moon.

Forester spotted a figure moving inside the trailer. A dark shadow across the window.

Cameron paused, staring.

His mind was moving quickly. If Artemis was right, then this man had found his daughter dead.

Marcy Thomas had taken her step-father's last name along with her mother and brothers, but Mattheus would still feel a bond with his daughter.

She'd died of an overdose.

And he'd blamed Julius Bateman for it.

And the others... So he'd started hunting their daughters. Started hunting everyone.

Forester frowned, considering all of this. Where had Mattheus gotten the money to hire the lawyers, the gunmen?

This wasn't just some serial killer. It was a full-blown conspiracy.

"Glass houses..." Forester muttered under his breath to himself.

He'd tracked down a murderer for the death of his wife.

Could he really blame Mattheus for doing the same because of his daughter's death?

But he hadn't stopped with Julius. He'd killed young women. Killed others.

Had nearly killed Artemis.

Forester's eyes narrowed as he remembered the shootout in the underpass.

And then, a split second passed, and he was nearly shot.

A bright flash of light, a *crack* from the window. And a bullet skimmed off the sand, kicking dust against his legs.

No sooner had the first shot missed than Forester's instincts took over.

He bolted for cover, moving fast, allowing the shadows from the bluff to cover his form. Even five steps into his dead sprint, Forester only just realized the direction of the gunfire.

The trailer.

He'd been spotted. His mind flitted to Artemis, fear for her safety rising within him, but he didn't slow.

Couldn't.

He kept moving, panting heavily, head low.

More gunshots.

He spotted the figure in the trailer moving now, trying to race to the door of the small, thin aluminum walls.

For the moment, the only cover Forester *had* was the trailer itself. He'd sprinted to the right, out of the line of sight from the window.

But eventually, the gunman would throw open the door and Forester would have nowhere to hide on the open beach.

So instead of turning to retreat, he made the only choice he could.

The door began to open.

A gun pointed out. A bullet with Forester's name on it was chambered.

He took the final few lunging strides, covering the distance in a blur.

He lowered his shoulder.

The gun aimed.

And instead of running away. Instead of diving for cover.

Forester slammed *into* the cover.

His shoulder into the metal of the thin-framed, small trailer. He felt like the old days, practicing at the gym, beating up on red, cushioned dummies.

Pain exploded down Forester's arm as he careened into the thin wall. The wheels on the ground rocked, the rubber lifting off.

The man inside the trailer yelped in surprise as he was sent stumbling backward.

The trailer tipped, and Forester shoved his full frame into the mobile home.

There were men, he knew, who could lift entire cars, or drag semi-trucks behind them. Forester wasn't nearly so strong.

Instead, he'd made sure to shove off the top of the metal frame, using his momentum to tip the trailer.

And then, the weight of the vehicle did the rest.

As he leaned into it, it almost seemed to get lighter.

Then it toppled completely, falling onto its side with a calamitous *crash*!

Artemis heard frightened breathing from further up the cliff where she had been sneaking around.

She didn't call out, though. Sticking to her training.

Good. They'd make an agent of her yet.

Now, Forester moved silently along the side of the overturned trailer.

He heard groaning from inside. A cough. The sound of scraping.

He clambered up on top of the trailer, gun in hand, and he shouted. "Come out with your hands up, or I'll shoot! FBI! Mattheus! Come on out!"

There was the sound of groaning from inside. But it wasn't a masculine voice.

A female was whimpering in pain.

Forester frowned.

He shifted uncomfortably, crouched on top of the toppled trailer, near one of the windows.

And then he glanced off to the side.

At the base of the cliff, he spotted a low glow from dim headlights.

An abandoned car sat there, the front door flung open. As if whoever had been in the vehicle hadn't bothered to close the doors.

It was a bright green Lamborghini.

A very fast car.

The sort of car that might make the whining engine sound they'd heard back at the Thomas' mansion.

And then, peering through the window, he spotted a flutter of red hair. A pale face. Wide eyes.

A woman clutching at her arm where she lay on the ground, groaning.

"Mrs. Thomas?" he said, startled.

She was glaring daggers at him. Her face had gone through a transformation.

This wasn't the docile, meek housewife she'd pretended to be around her new husband and her twin sons.

There was a ferocious glare in those eyes. In one hand, she clutched a pistol that she'd been using to shoot at Cameron.

He kept his gun trained on the red-haired woman. "Don't move," he said, eight feet above her, crouched by the window, aiming his gun through the shattered glass.

"You're ruining everything!" she snarled at him.

"Where is he? Where's your ex?"

Her lip was bleeding, and she didn't speak.

"Let me guess?" Forester said. "You want to lawyer up, huh? Just like your goons. They're yours, right? You and your ex-husband. You're behind all of this."

She didn't speak.

"Where is he?" Forester demanded again.

He could hear hurried footsteps now, and glanced back to spot Artemis racing towards him, her eyes wide in horror at the scene.

Forester perched on top of the toppled trailer, like some stone gargoyle watching a gothic church.

But he returned his attention to the would-be shooter. Her arm looked broken.

Otherwise, he guessed she might have tried to aim at him once more.

"You'll never find him!" she snarled.

Forester nodded. "You're right. We won't. Not until you tell us where he is."

The woman's glare intensified and her lip curled into a sneer. But she said nothing. Then, her hand twitched.

Forester didn't blink but fired twice.

Each shot striking the aluminum at her side.

"Next one is in your head," he said, "if you try to raise that gun again. Drop it. Now!"

He wasn't demanding. His voice spoke matter-of-factly.

She stared up at him, hesitant, trembling.

But then she swallowed, and her hand loosened its grip. The gun tumbled onto the metal wall where she lay in her topsy-turvy trailer.

Gasping, she slowly dragged herself to her feet. Her eyes glaring at Cameron.

"What's going on?" Artemis finally called out, having determined the gunshots were over.

"Mrs. Thomas," Forester called back, his gaze still fixated on their suspect. "She came to warn her ex-husband."

"Mattheus isn't here?"

"No." Forester returned his attention to the red-haired beauty.

The woman was now rising to her feet, wincing as she did, her features pinched and pale.

She glared up at Cameron, shivering where she stood.

Forester returned her glare. Her head was now only a couple of feet below him. She looked as if she'd risen just to get a better look at where he crouched above her, in what now seemed like a skylight only a couple of feet above her head.

"You don't know what you're meddling with," she warned, her voice hoarse and pained.

Forester just shrugged. "Tell us where he is. Where's Kayla?"

But now, she snickered. "Kayla? Really? That bitch is going to be the crowning achievement. Her dad caused this. Her father caused all of this!" she yelled now, her eyes bright and quite mad. "I hope he guts her. I hope he peels her like a grape!"

All signs of a content housewife had been shattered. All that remained was pure vengeance and loathing.

"Because Julius dealt the drugs that killed your daughter?"

She sneered up at him, hands limp at her side. Blood trickling down the corner of her mouth.

"You don't know anything, do you?"

"Because Julius was sleeping with your daughter!" Artemis called out from where she stood at the base of the trailer, her feet pressed in cold sand.

The water continued to swish around them.

Now, Mrs. Thomas went still, staring.

"Who is that?" she called out, hesitant.

"It's true, isn't it?" Artemis called back, her voice echoing because of the acoustics caused by the towering bluff.

No response.

"It is," Artemis said. "Julius knew your daughter's age. Exactly. Twenty-four, he said. Why would the distant, cold father of a girl he didn't seem to care much about know such a personal detail about a young, beautiful woman? A woman who had access to his stash. A woman who was seen with an older man, arguing at a bar where only the wealthy and the elite show up!"

As Artemis rattled this off, Forester stared at her, impressed.

Mrs. Thomas just remained silent, her eyes narrowed, fury in her gaze.

Then, she looked up at Cameron and said in a low whisper, "You can't stop it. They're all going to get what's coming to them. They're going to pay."

"Who?" Forester said slowly. "Who's going to get it?"

She just smiled now, flashing teeth, looking very much like a shark.

"Who are you targeting? Who's *they*?"

But now she started to giggle, her voice warbling like some deranged songbird. She shook her head furiously and wagged a finger from side to side.

"Don't you wish you knew," she murmured. "But that's for me to know and you to find out. Now, *lawyer*."

Forester stared down at her.

"Did you hear me?" she snapped, reaching up to wipe a droplet of blood away. "Lawyer. Now!"

Forester hesitated briefly, studying her. He didn't move.

"Well?" she said, jutting out her sharp chin, her eyelashes fluttering imperiously, her red hair fluttering, caught by a gust of breeze through the shattered window.

It took Forester a moment to make up his mind. When he did, he said, "You know... I'm already under investigation. There's some powerful folk who want me in trouble."

She blinked, her nose wrinkling, her brow furrowed in some amount of confusion as if she wasn't quite sure why he was telling her this.

Forester said. "No lawyer. You tell me where your ex is. Tell me where Kayla is. Who are you targeting? I'm not going to let you kill another."

His mind flickered back to another time. A woman almost the same age as Whitney Martin. At the time, he'd failed to help her.

Not again.

"I said *lawyer*!" she screeched.

"Tell me where Kayla is! Tell me who you're targeting!"

"All of them! They'll all die! And you can't stop it! It's already happening. I hope Kayla screams. I hope they do things to her before killing her. I'd like to watch if I could. I hope she sobs so loudly that—"

Then Mrs. Thomas screeched.

This was on account of what Cameron had done.

Forester's hand had shot through the window and grabbed a tangle of her red hair, bunching it around his fist like a fighter's wrap.

And then he yanked, hauling her bodily out of the toppled trailer.

She screamed as he flung the woman over the side of the trailer.

She landed in the sand, her breath whooshing from her lungs.

Artemis let out a little gasp next to him.

Forester hopped off the toppled trailer, landing in the sand next to his suspect, gun still clutched in hand.

He could picture her mismatched eyes. Her smile. He'd killed a man on a beach not too different from this one.

Though that one had been lined with palm trees, and it had been a sunny day.

But the scent of the salt water, the indenting sand...

It all reminded him of what he'd lost. And what he'd taken in return.

He wouldn't lose another.

He was going to find Kayla, reward or not.

He loomed over Mrs. Thomas, where she lay in the sand, spluttering, crawling back, shimmying against the ground.

But he stalked her down, pointing the gun at her now. "Tell me where he is."

"Cameron!" Artemis called out. "Don't! Think what you're doing!"

He ignored her cries. Another flash of mismatched eyes. Not Artemis. Another love.

"I said tell me where he is! Where's Kayla! Who are you targeting next?" His voice boomed in the open space, competing with the churning waves.

"I don't know!"

"Tell me!"

"No!"

Forester fired twice. Both bullets hitting the sand next to her. She yelped with each shot.

"Cameron, don't!" Artemis pleaded. She was now at his side, tugging at his arm.

But Forester shook his head. "No. No, she doesn't get to lawyer up. Not like the others. We're doing it my way."

Artemis said, "I know where he is. Or... or I know how to find him!"

Forester paused, frowned, then glanced at her.

She was holding a phone in one hand, displaying it so he could see.

"Wh-what?"

"It's her phone!" Artemis said quickly. "She was trying to call someone. It was still unlocked!"

Now, Mrs. Thomas was gaping at the device. And a look of horror appeared in her eyes.

Forester said, "Check the most recent numbers."

Artemis was nodding, and she looked relieved that the gun was no longer pointed towards their surrendered suspect.

Artemis hesitated briefly, then said, "Six calls from the same number in the last two days. Other calls on the same days our victims disappeared. It all started the day that Mrs. Thomas' daughter died."

"Call it," Forester said.

Artemis hesitated. "We might only have one shot to find out where he is."

"Do it," Forester said. "We don't have time to set up a tap. You need to get him to give you his location."

She stared at him.

"He won't."

241

"He will."

"Why would he?"

"Because," Forester said quietly, glancing back towards the woman on the sand. She was crying now. "We have the only person left in the world that he still loves. Why else would she go this far? Hmm? He'll want her back."

"We... we can't hurt her," Artemis said softly.

"He doesn't know that." And Forester didn't say this part, but inwardly, he was also thinking that *he* didn't know that either.

They needed to find where Mattheus had holed up. Needed to find who he was targeting, and where Bateman's daughter was.

By the sound of things, they were going to kill more than one person next. A spree? A mass murder?

He shivered at the thought.

"Call him, please."

Artemis nodded briefly, inhaled as if to steel herself, then placed the call.

Chapter 25

"Hello, Mattheus," Artemis Blythe said softly into the cell phone. He hadn't answered yet; she was just practicing. Trying to keep as calm as possible. She did her best to sound calm, but inside, her heart was racing. This man had killed a young woman, attempted to kill another, and had stabbed his own daughter to make her overdose look like a murder. She would have to tread lightly to get what they wanted.

"Who the hell is this?" came the gruff reply from the other end of the line.

"That's not important," Artemis said, her voice catching for a moment. "But this phone... you know whose it is, don't you?"

"Where is my wife?"

"She's your ex, isn't she?" Artemis said conversationally. This was more a dig than anything, but the more distracted he was, the better.

"I want to speak with her!" he snapped.

"I'm afraid that can't happen. I need to know where you are, sir. We can end this peaceably."

"You didn't take Tammy peaceably, I'll tell you that right now. Tammy! Hey, TAMMY, are you there!"

"I'm here!" Mrs. Thomas called out, her voice strained. "Don't listen to them! Don't do it!"

A pause. "Why does she sound scared?" the voice whispered. "Who the hell is this?"

"FBI," Artemis replied. "I'd like to help end this, Mattheus."

"You can't help me."

"Maybe not," Artemis said, doing her best to remain collected, "but I can offer you a way out. A way to end things."

There was a long pause on the other end of the line. "What kind of way out?"

She could tell by his tone that he wasn't considering the offer but, rather, searching for his own solution. Stalling.

She felt herself frown.

She glanced again where Forester was standing gun in hand. He nodded encouragingly at her, but she simply couldn't bring herself to use a human being as a bargaining chip.

She sighed, hesitant.

Then Forester stepped in, swiped the phone before she could protest, and barked into it. "If you turn yourself in, we can make sure your ex is safe. If not... I can't promise anything nice happens to her."

He raised his weapon and fired it at the water three times.

"What the hell was that!" the man on the phone yelled in horror. "What was that? Tammy? Tammy, are you okay?" His voice echoed over the speaker.

Forester's expression remained dark. "Where are you?" he snapped.

Another long pause. Artemis held her breath, not sure if she should intervene. But after a few moments, Mattheus finally spoke.

"How do I know you won't hurt her?" His voice had softened slightly, and there was a hint of emotion in his tone.

"You don't," Forester said. "But I can promise you she won't be hurt if you tell us where you are. We can help end this. Where are you? Where's Kayla?"

Silence. Artemis watched her partner, tense. Finally, after what seemed like an eternity, the gruff voice returned.

"Okay," Mattheus said softly. "You want to play this game? I'll tell you exactly where I am. It's too late. We timed it. Police won't arrive in time. My men are only five minutes out."

"Five minutes from where?" Cameron demanded.

"Vengeance," the voice said quietly. "Tammy," it said, louder. "I love you. Are you okay?"

"Where are you?" Forester demanded, even louder. "Don't make me do something we'll both regret." His voice was a snarl, and Artemis wondered if Mattheus could hear something in Forester's voice that scared him, because a moment later, he said, "You want me? I need assurances that she'll be safe. Let her go."

"Not a chance."

"Do it, and I'll tell you where I am."

"No dice. You'll lie."

"Then bring her to me. I'll kill Kayla unless you bring her to me."

Forester paused. "Where are you?"

"Did you hear me? I said—"

"I heard you!" Forester snapped. "We can trade. Your ex for Kayla. If you hurt her, though, I'll do the same to you. Got it?"

"So dramatic." A long, weary sigh. "It's too late anyway. I'm at a burnt mansion in an old, abandoned lot. Do you know where *Biggie's Small* is? It's a shitty hole-in-the-wall country club joint. I'll be here for another ten minutes, then I'm gone. If you come with backup... if you come with *anyone*, and if you've hurt my wife in any way, Kayla is dead. Is that clear? You better hurry."

The line went dead. Forester gripped the phone tightly.

Artemis felt her heart pounding in her chest. She stared at Cameron wide-eyed.

He returned her look, his expression grim.

"What was he talking about?" Forester said. "That it was too late? His guys were five minutes away?"

He addressed these questions towards Mrs. Thomas, but the woman ignored them, staring away from him.

Forester frowned even more deeply. Artemis could feel her nerves twisting about.

"We should go," she whispered. "He said he'd only stay for another few minutes. We might not get there in time anyway."

"You know where the burnt mansion is, don't you?" Forester snapped, glaring at Tammy.

The woman hesitated, glanced at the phone in his hand, and a flash of hope crossed her face. She nodded once.

"Good," Forester said. "I'm driving. Give directions. Or else."

He turned now, and Artemis began to move. They hastened towards the green sports vehicle that had been left under the bluff near the trailer.

Or else...

Those words didn't just apply to Mrs. Thomas.

Artemis felt as if the threat were directed at all of them.

Time was out.

And she didn't even know what for.

CHAPTER 26

ARTEMIS' HEART POUNDED AS she approached the burnt husk of the old, abandoned mansion.

The towering structure was like some shadow, rising from the earth.

Part of the ceiling had caved in. A porch was missing. Walls were scorched and stained with dark soot.

The ground around the enormous structure was also streaked with ash, and nothing grew in the gardens.

Forester and Artemis moved side-by-side, approaching the structure.

Their prisoner remained back in the car, locked in the back seat, her hands and feet cuffed.

"See anything?" Forester whispered as they approached the darkened building.

"No."

"Think he's got us chasing our tails?"

Artemis felt her stomach twist. This, indeed, was a fear of hers. "I don't know," she whispered back.

The sky matched the hue of the structure as darkness came in quickly. As they approached the front entrance, Artemis felt a chill run down her spine. She couldn't shake off the feeling that they were being watched.

The old wooden door creaked as Forester pushed it open. The sound echoed throughout the abandoned mansion.

The inside of the mansion was even more eerie than the outside. Cobwebs covered every corner, and the air was thick with dust. The only light came from the small flashlight Forester was holding.

"If I tell you to run, you run, got it?" Forester whispered. "Let's take the first floor then check the second."

Artemis nodded, and they moved slowly. As they drifted down a hall, the floorboards creaked beneath her feet. She couldn't help but wonder what secrets this mansion was hiding.

Were they being tricked?

Was this even a known place to Mattheus, or had he sent them here out of spite?

Forester occasionally checked his phone, making sure the GPS of his car was stationary. He had the keys with him, and they'd parked far enough away to keep the vehicle out of sight.

Most of the first floor was empty, abandoned. Walls were missing in entire sections, other portions were showing signs of water damage where the fire had evidently been doused.

The second floor was just as dark and musty as the first. Artemis shone her flashlight around the hallway, noting the peeling wallpaper and faded photographs. She came to a door that was slightly ajar and pushed it open.

Inside, they found a bedroom. The bed was little more than rusted springs, and there was no sign of anyone living there. Artemis was about to leave the room when she heard a faint noise coming from the closet.

She paused.

Another sound.

Forester nudged her, and she nodded to show she'd heard it as well.

She took a deep breath and slowly approached the closet, Forester at her side.

Then, from inside the closet, there came a voice.

"This is where Kayla was being kept," the voice said, crackling.

Artemis and Forester both froze.

Forester, gun in hand, reached out and flung open the closet door.

A radio receiver was sitting on a charred, three-legged stool.

"Hello there," a voice said, coming from the speaker.

Artemis whirled around and noticed the camera over the door, pointed in their direction. She glanced back and spotted a shattered window behind the rusted bed.

The voice was tutting on the radio. "Now... I told you to come alone. I don't see any backup, but where's my wife?"

"Ex-wife," Forester said, and Artemis guessed he added this just to insult the man.

There was a wounded pause over the radio.

Artemis kept glancing around the burned and abandoned room, searching for any sign of danger. Prickles erupted up her spine.

"So where are you, Mattie," Forester said, glaring at the radio receiver. "Do you want your wife back, or not?"

There was a pause. A faint swallow. Artemis almost thought she heard a fragment of emotion in the man's voice as he said, "It won't matter anyway. I just wanted to tell you myself... You're both about to die. Kayla is in the basement. But the entire building is rigged to blow." A long, weary sigh. "Oh well. It had to end eventually. Five... Four... Three..."

As soon as he hit *three*, Forester's eyes widened in horror. He moved fast as thought.

Artemis stumbled as he wrapped an arm around her waist. He took two lunging steps.

Two... One...

Then flung them both through the window with a shout.

And then...

BOOOM!

CHAPTER 27

AN ENORMOUS ERUPTION. A fireball chased them out of the window with searing heat as they tumbled head over heels.

Artemis hit the ground hard, her body aching from the fall. She groaned as she tried to push herself up, but Forester's weight was on top of her, and she couldn't move. She felt him breathing heavily against her neck, but he wasn't moving. Wasn't speaking.

Smoke and ash were now billowing out of the mansion's window. An entire section of the house collapsed with a groan, wooden beams protesting.

"Forester?" she called out, her voice shaky. "Are you okay?"

There was no response. Artemis tried to turn her head, but his weight was too heavy. She was trapped beneath him, and she couldn't see anything. She could hear the sound of sirens in the distance, and she knew they had to move fast.

"Forester, we need to get out of here," she said urgently, trying to push him off her.

But Forester didn't move. Artemis felt a cold sense of dread wash over her. She tried to force herself out from underneath him, but it was no use.

Suddenly, she felt something warm and wet against her neck. She froze, realizing it was blood.

"Forester, please!" she cried out, her voice desperate.

She managed to pull herself free, gasping as she did. Forester's head was bleeding. He must've struck it when jumping from the window. Now, she groaned, wincing as bits of splinters and glass tumbled from her.

She tried to brush it off, breathing heavily as she did.

"Forester?" She gingerly probed at his cheek.

He was still breathing. His eyes fluttered, but then he let out a faint groan.

Sirens were still approaching.

Cameron was semi-conscious on the ground.

He was much larger than her, but the heat was spreading, the smoke billowing. She had to pull him away from the blaze.

But even as she realized this, she remembered what Mattheus had said.

Kayla was still in there.

Artemis glanced back at the burning mansion, tensed, desperately trying to reach a decision.

Then, she bent double, snatched at Forester's arms, and let out a mighty gasp as she tried to pull the large, muscled man towards the treeline.

He was still not speaking, still unconscious.

Artemis grunted with effort as she dragged Forester's heavy body through the grass towards the safety of the trees. The smoke was thickening around them, making it difficult to see. She could hear the crackling of the flames as they consumed the remains of the mansion. She had to get Forester far enough away from the inferno to treat his injuries properly.

As she pulled him along, her mind raced. Mattheus had said that Kayla was still inside the burning building. Artemis couldn't leave her there to die. She had to go back in and find her.

But how? The heat was too intense, and the flames were spreading rapidly. She couldn't risk going in without a plan.

Then she remembered the basement. Mattheus had said that Kayla was in the basement. It was possible that she was still alive but trapped.

Artemis made a split-second decision. She couldn't leave Kayla behind, even if it meant risking her own life. She had to try to save her.

A sacrifice. Sometimes, to win the game, a valuable piece had to be traded off the board.

Artemis was that piece.

Forester was out of commission. It was all down to her. In a way, this didn't scare her nearly as much as the upcoming FBI field test or the investigation by Harmony Schmidt.

There simply wasn't enough time *to* fear.

She pulled Forester as close to the trees as possible and then turned back towards the burning mansion. The heat was blistering, and the smoke was making it hard to breathe. But Artemis gritted her teeth and pushed forward, determined to find Kayla.

She made her way through the burning debris, her heart pounding with fear and adrenaline. The flames were everywhere, but she remained focused, scanning the wreckage for any sign of the young woman.

The flames of the burning mansion were raging, sweat prickling on her face as she peered through the open threshold.

So far, the fire hadn't spread to the lower level. Though it was eating at the floorboards and moving along the ceiling.

Soon, the whole building might collapse, and Artemis was worried that it might all be too late. Smoke filled the air, thick and oppressive, and the walls of the house were slowly engulfed in flames that crackled and rose higher. Artemis took a deep breath and stepped forward, her feet crunching on the burning floorboards as she inched her way in.

She quickly looked around, hoping to catch a glimpse of the young woman she was looking for, but all that greeted her was the overpowering heat and the roar of the flames. Artemis brushed away the ash that clung to her face and hair, trying to stay alert.

The fire had spread throughout the mansion, and it was impossible to tell where it started or where it was headed next. All around her, furniture was burning, books were aflame, and walls were crumbling. Each step was a risk, as a floorboard could give way or a ceiling could collapse.

She tried to stay focused, but it was difficult with the smoke and flames swirling around her.

She kept her sweater up over her face, trying to keep low to avoid inhaling smoke.

She'd once read that most victims in fires died from smoke inhalation.

She continued forward, half crouched, gasping into her sweater.

Come on... she thought. She needed a little help. Needed Kayla to say something. *Do* something.

She continued forward, down a small hall, the crackling blaze oppressive.

She had to turn back.

Her back was seared now. Her breath was scarcely coming. She couldn't keep going. She had to turn around.

Suddenly she heard a faint cry, and she snapped her head up. It was coming from the end of this hall, near an open doorway leading to wooden steps. Artemis pressed on, and she moved quickly, trying to keep her footing as she descended the wooden staircase. It creaked and groaned beneath her weight, and she had to jump over sections that had already collapsed.

When she reached the basement floor, Artemis heard the cry again, louder this time. She followed it to a back room, near an old, copper water heater, the heat intensifying as she got closer.

And then...

A flood of relief.

Emotion.

She nearly gasped but then broke into choking breaths. She regained her composure, staring at the figure huddled in the room.

A young woman chained to the wall, her voice hoarse from screaming. "Please!" the woman gasped, her eyes bright with tears. "Please, help!"

Artemis rushed to her, but the metal cuffs were too strong to be broken by hand. Artemis quickly scanned the room, searching for something to use to smash the links. Her eyes landed on a metal pipe near the window, and she grabbed it. With all her might, she bashed the pipe against the handcuffs.

Sparks flew. The pipe struck the cuffs again and again.

Then, the cuffs shattered, and Kayla let out a desperate gasp.

The smoke was getting thicker and the flames were getting higher. There was no time to waste. Artemis grabbed the woman, who was now free, and dragged her out of the room and up the stairs. She was coughing and struggling to breathe, and Artemis had to half-carry her.

Kayla leaned heavily on Artemis, half collapsed. Artemis kept going, unable to stop, unable to slow. Everything depended on her ability to *keep* going.

Her shoulder sagged under the weight of the small, young woman.

And then...

Ahead of her, the ceiling collapsed, cutting off her escape route.

Artemis let out a cry, stumbling back. Fire seared her calf, and she yelped, trying to avoid the blaze in the hall.

But now, their path was cut off. Sparks erupted from where the floor had fallen through.

Nowhere to go.

Kayla was saying something, her voice weak, but Artemis couldn't make out the words.

Panic now flared in her mind.

They were trapped.

They were going to burn alive.

The jutting, ashen teeth of lumber and floorboards flickered with orange and angry red, spitting ash and fumes, blocking her path like a host of sentries armed with flaming spears.

They had to find another way. But where?

Her mind was reeling. Too much smoke. Pain in her calf. Was her pant leg on fire?

Dammit. Think! Think!

Kayla was moaning. Then quiet. Had she breathed too much smoke?

Was Artemis now carrying a dead girl?

No... No, she was speaking. Barely a murmur, still leaning heavily on Artemis. But she was saying something.

And this time, Artemis caught the words. "*Window*..." Faint. So very faint. But Artemis turned, and in a brief second, she spotted it.

There, through the adjoining dining room, over a burning table.

A large window.

A spark of hope.

A window was still intact. The window was closed, so the oxygen hadn't rushed in to churn up more flames. The moment she opened it, the greedy fire would snarl and snap towards the breeze.

But it was the only way out.

Artemis rushed forward, hauling Kayla with her, her entire body aching from carrying the younger woman. She set her down below the window, and then she pulled the chair next to them, using it as a step.

She had to be quick.

The window was small, just enough for one person to fit through.

Artemis turned back to Kayla, her eyes pleading.

"I'm sorry, I have to do this," she said, her voice barely audible over the roar of the flames.

And then, in one swift motion, she dragged at the young woman. Kayla groaned but pushed with her legs, helping Artemis lift her. And then, Artemis set her through the window.

The smoke was getting thicker, and the heat was unbearable.

Artemis took a deep breath, paused.

And then the floor fell through, taking the dining room table with it.

She jumped... A split second before.

Just in time.

As the house collapsed. As the fire swallowed the wood, and hungrily grasped at her, she leapt through the window with a desperate shout, and hit the ground, rolling onto the grass outside.

She tumbled a few times, her calf still aching, rolling on her previously injured hand. She lay there, panting and coughing, the night sky twinkling above her.

Artemis looked up at the burning building, her heart pounding.

"We made it," Artemis whispered to no one at all.

She crawled in the grass, moving away from the swirling smoke, gasping and coughing. Kayla, now away from the blaze, looked still somewhat conscious, though her head was slumped.

She was sitting in the grass, head dipped and staring towards Artemis.

"Thank you," the young woman whispered. And then tears began pouring down her face. She was sobbing, crying horribly. "Thank you!" Kayla said, louder.

Artemis felt a lump in her throat. She stumbled to her feet, still moving away from the burning structure.

A part of her knew with some certainty that the look of relief on Kayla's face was worth far more than all the money in the world.

But the relief was short-lived.

Kayla let out a strangled breath, sobbed a final time, and then, her voice quavering, she said, "You..." She swallowed, drawing air again and trying once more with a sturdier voice, "You have to help them. They're going to kill them all."

"What? Who?" Artemis said.

Kayla was shaking her head, tears still streaming. "The estates. The gated community. Gunmen... so many guns... golden masks!"

And then, Kayla's eyes fluttered, and though she tried, she couldn't speak further.

She stumbled back, collapsing in the grass, completely unconscious.

Gunmen... Kill them all...

The gated community.

And suddenly, it all made sense.

The people Mattheus blamed for his daughter's death. For the relationship between Mr. Bateman and his daughter.

Money. Drugs. Power.

The billionaires' coastal gated community was the target.

Horror welled up in Artemis as she realized they were likely already too late.

CHAPTER 28

ARTEMIS WAS SHAKING AS she and Forester drove up the long, winding road. Cameron had recovered, but was wincing every few seconds, and constantly reaching for his ribs. Occasionally he'd rub at his head, where she spotted a nasty gash. She kept glancing in his direction, as if to make sure he was alright.

But there was simply no time. Ahead of them, a tall, spiked gate marked the entrance to the billionaires' exclusive community. But the sight that greeted them was not one of opulence and protection.

Five masked gunmen, dressed head-to-toe in black, blocked the gate. The gunmen had heavy guns in hand and golden masks on their faces. They had barricaded themselves behind a row of black jeeps.

Further in the gated community, just within the entrance, Artemis spotted three men in white uniforms.

All of them laying in pools of blood, eyes staring up, sightlessly at the sky.

The security guards.

Dead.

And in the distance, through the bars, Artemis spotted other masked gunmen moving through the billionaires' homes.

Shots rang out. Screams echoed.

They had arrived in time to witness a massacre.

Forester was cursing as they peeled up the road. And now, Artemis understood the point of the rigged explosions at the burnt mansion. It had drawn law enforcement away. They wouldn't be able to respond to the rampage before it was all too late.

Only Forester and Artemis faced the gunmen.

"Brace yourself," Forester muttered.

Her stomach tightened, and her eyes widened, staring ahead as they picked up speed, their car serving as a battering ram as they revved towards the gate.

Suddenly, the gunmen raised weapons. Frowning.

Perhaps they'd been expecting reinforcements, but now they seemed to realize something was off.

"Go! Go!" Artemis was yelling. She couldn't think of any other word. Adrenaline was pumping, and her mind was racing. Mr. Mattheus and Mrs. Thomas had used their combined funds to hire these gunmen, most likely. Or had recruited other disenfranchised sorts. Artemis wasn't sure what billionaires got up to in their spare time. The golden masks and overdramatic spectacle made her think of some secret society of killers.

But none of the speculation mattered as they hurtled like a comet towards the gunfire.

Bullets slammed into the windshield.

"Get low!" Forester screamed.

As the windshield spiderwebbed from the bullet impacts, Artemis had already ducked.

The two of them kept their heads down, but Forester was still flooring the gas pedal.

Artemis winced, anticipating the collision.

One of the tires blew out.

They nearly veered off course, but Forester yanked the steering wheel, keeping them back on track, and then...

CRASH!

They slammed through the jeep barricade, and screams went suddenly silent as men were tossed like rag dolls.

The momentum of their collision brought them careening through the gates.

Artemis' head whipped forward, striking the dashboard, *hard*.

She saw stars for a moment and tasted copper in her mouth. But the adrenaline rush dulled the pain. She shook her head to clear it, and her eyes flicked up to the rearview mirror.

The gunmen were regaining their footing, and Artemis saw a flash of movement as one of them raised their gun again.

"Forester!" she shouted.

He didn't need prompting. He had already slammed the car in reverse, and they were backing up just as the gunman opened fire.

Bullets pinged off the car, and Forester swerved erratically, trying to avoid the shots.

Artemis reached behind the seat, her fingers fumbling as she searched for Forester's spare weapon.

She felt a cold metal object in her hand and pulled it out.

It was the gun. The pistol still felt strange in her hand outside the training range, but the weight of it was comforting.

"Use it!" Forester shouted, noticing the weapon. His hands were glued to the steering wheel.

Her window was already shattered, so there was no need to roll it down as she peeked up and over, took a deep breath, and aimed.

Forester was now swerving back through the gate, trying to keep the gunmen distracted.

She spotted a man by the bumper of the crushed jeep, taking aim.

She winced.

No time to think. No time to sympathize. Sympathy cut both ways. Not just for the gunman, but also for Forester, for all the people *inside* the gated community.

A horrible, horrible decision.

She hated having to make it.

She squeezed the trigger, and the recoil nearly knocked her back.

She missed. Bullets ricocheted off the hood of the car.

Forester slowed suddenly. "Again! Squeeze, aim through!"

His voice echoed, reminding her of the training they'd completed together. She tried again, now that they were moving slower.

This time, she hit her target.

The gunman fell to the ground, clutching his leg. Two other men in masks were lying on the ground where Forester had slammed into them.

Another was missing.

But there were still more gunmen inside the compound. More gunshots resounding in the air, followed by screams of pain or pleading.

Forester hit the gas, and they limped away from the scene on their battered vehicle, leaving the chaos behind as they rushed *into* the gated community.

Artemis's heart was still pounding in her chest.

Suddenly, ahead, Artemis spotted a window smash. A rifle barrel jutted out of the window, aiming towards her.

Forester cursed, pulling the steering wheel sharply, "Out!" he yelled.

They skidded to a stop, and he reached across her, shoving open her door.

She didn't hesitate as gunfire erupted.

Artemis lurched out of the car, her legs suddenly weak. As gunshots cracked in the air, she scrambled to her feet and tried to run for cover. But an ornamental, far-too-early Christmas tree was the only refuge she had—and so she dashed behind it, heart pounding, trying to keep herself as small as possible.

Forester had already leapt out of the car, his gun raised. He fired twice, hitting two of the gunmen in the window before they had a chance to shoot. The remaining shooter, however, was already turning his rifle on the two of them, firing. Artemis heard the bullets whizzing past her head and felt the air rush as they passed.

She crouched lower, trembling, behind the tree and waited for Forester's orders. He shot off two more rounds, then motioned for her to stay low and try to make her way around the tree. Artemis scurried forward, her eyes darting from side to side, ready to dive for cover again if necessary.

They had to stall for the cops to show up.

How many people were here?

No way of knowing.

They had to find Mattheus.

Cut off the head of the snake, and the body would perish.

They had to find the orchestrator of all of this.

Mrs. Thomas had been left back outside the bombed mansion, chained to a tree, waiting for the cops to show up.

They'd left their leverage behind.

But now, talking was over.

A second shooter emerged in the window, pulling at the arm of the first, muttering something in his ear. The gunmen stopped firing for a moment, and the air was silent save for the distant honking of car horns. But then one of them shouted something in a voice too muffled to make out. More shots rang out. One bullet grazed a tree near Artemis, sending splinters flying.

Forester fired another shot, but this time it was met with a barrage of bullets. Forester and Artemis both ducked low, flattening themselves against the ground. Forester grabbed Artemis's arm and pulled her forward suddenly.

"Go!"

They sprinted towards the side of the mansion, hoping to use the structure itself for cover.

The gunmen kept firing. Bullets thunked into the faux stone siding, one after another, sending chips of plasticine flying. Artemis gasped, the ringing of gunfire in her ears.

"We have to find Mattheus," she whispered fiercely as the two of them now crouched next to a coiled garden hose, once again reminding herself of the snake metaphor in her mind.

"No clue where he is," Forester shot back.

Artemis looked around.

She spotted two figures across the lawn, hiding behind a garden shed. An elderly couple, both of them trembling, tears in their eyes.

Artemis held a finger to her lips, shushing them. They just stared at her, panicked.

And then, behind them, Artemis spotted two more gunmen slowly slinking forward. So far, the elderly couple and the gunmen hadn't spotted each other, as a hedge divided them, but within a few steps, the couple would come into the gunmen's sights.

Artemis knew she had to act fast. She signaled to Forester, who nodded in understanding. They both sprang out from behind the garden hose, guns raised, and screamed at the elderly couple to get down. The couple obeyed, and the gunmen turned towards them, caught off guard. Forester fired a shot that grazed one of the gunmen's shoulders, causing him to stumble back. The other raised his gun, but Artemis shot him before he had a chance to fire. Her stomach twisted as he hit the ground, but there was no time for emotions. Not right now.

The couple was safe, but they were still in the middle of a firefight. Artemis and Forester had to keep moving. They ran towards the nearest mansion, where most of the noise was coming from, weaving between garden beds and dodging behind statues. Forester led the way, his gun held out in front of him. Artemis followed close behind, her eyes scanning their surroundings for any sign of danger.

As they reached the mansion, they could hear gunfire coming from inside. They moved towards the entrance.

A man like Mattheus would want to be the center of attention.

He'd planned for this. The melodrama was his creation. The stupid masks, the convoluted plans...

He was going to be in here.

He had to be.

They entered hurriedly, the sounds of gunfire coming from further down the hall.

The mansion was in shambles. Glass shards and debris littered the ground, and the air was thick with the smell of smoke. Artemis and Forester moved cautiously through the halls, checking each room for any sign of Mattheus or the remaining gunmen.

As they turned a corner, they suddenly froze.

A thin, gaunt-faced man was striding back and forth in front of a group of sobbing figures. Two men, two women, all of them with heads stooped.

"You knew what he was doing..." the gaunt-faced man was saying. He looked something like an emaciated skeleton. His skin stretched across his bones. His chin was so sharp, she thought it might cut something.

Two other gunmen were also facing the group, aiming semi-automatic rifles at the figures kneeling on the luxurious carpet.

The gunfire had faded now, and bullets riddled the wall behind the kneeling figures.

Clearly, Mattheus was enjoying the opportunity to play with his food. He seemed to enjoy the tears of his four sobbing victims.

And for the moment, it distracted him.

Artemis stood in the doorway, breathing heavily.

Mattheus was ranting now, waving his hands about like a conductor, spindly fingers like a conductor's wand. "You let him hide in plain sight. He met her here, didn't he? My daughter. She was half his age, and you didn't tell me, Markie, did you?"

The man, kneeling next to a woman Artemis presumed to be his wife tried to speak but was struck across the face by Mattheus' fist.

"Did I ask you to speak!" the grieving man screamed, spittle flecking the victim's face. "Did I? Hmm? Do you think I spent these months hiring these men? Planning this? Just to let *you* stop it? All of you are going to pay. I'm going to turn this all to rubble, Markie! Going to take your family, the way you all took mine!"

"We didn't know!" the man named Markie exclaimed, sobbing. "I didn't know what Bateman was doing. I didn't!"

"LIAR!"

Another strike.

This one sent the man reeling back, clutching at his face. His wife sobbed, and the two other figures crouched by them cringed.

Forester was already aiming.

He had a clear shot.

Artemis felt her stomach twinge.

But he was going to murder them all.

They needed Mattheus alive, though. To call off the rest of his men. To end this. To tell them if there were any other explosives...

And then...

As Forester's finger began to squeeze on the trigger.

Something cold brushed her neck.

"Drop it," said a voice. "Or I'll shoot the lady."

She froze. The cold metal item jammed against her neck even harder. "I said drop it, or I'll shot her."

Forester had gone still at these words. And he glanced over, swallowing slowly. Panic flared through Artemis.

CHAPTER 29

THE GUN JAMMED AGAINST her neck even harder, and Artemis felt her stomach twist.

"DROP it," the voice behind her demanded.

She glanced cautiously back, and her fears were realized as she spotted one of the golden-masked gunmen had snuck up behind them. The man was glaring at her, his eyes icy cold behind the mask.

She thought she detected a faint, Eastern European accent to his voice.

Forester slowly released his grip on his weapon, allowing it to clatter to the ground. The gunman jabbed at their necks. "Move!" he snapped, and then in a louder voice, he called out, "Look what I found, boss."

Dread filled Artemis' chest. Mattheus slowly turned to face them.

He grinned, his eyes alight with malice.

"Well, well," he said. "What have we here?"

He gestured to the two gunmen in the room, who seized hold of Artemis and Forester, pressing cold metal against their necks. The third gunman blocked the door.

Forester snarled, trying to reach for the hand gripping him.

"Do it, asshole, and I'll topple you!"

"Now, now," Mattheus said. "Let's not be too hasty. I'm sure we can work something out. After all, I'm a reasonable man."

Artemis and Forester exchanged a glance. Fear in both their eyes. The man kneeling on the ground, still bleeding from the nose, looked temporarily relieved that he was no longer the object of their focus.

Forester and Artemis were dragged further into the room towards Mattheus.

He was eyeing them both, his lips curled into a sneer, but there was hatred in his eyes.

"I've seen you around. Bateman hired you two to cover up what he was doing."

"That's not what happened," Artemis said.

But before she'd finished, his hand was already moving. His blow struck her across the cheek, and pain blossomed over her face.

She grimaced, leaning back.

Forester snarled and tried to intervene, but the two men pointed their guns at him.

The whimpering from the kneeling victims continued. Artemis could hear gunshots throughout the gated community, suggesting that the golden-masked henchmen were shooting the wealthy in their homes.

They had to take Mattheus out. To get him to call off the attack before everyone died.

But how?

They were disarmed. Guns were pointed at them both.

Forester kept trying to catch her eye, to see if she was okay, but her face was still stinging, her ear ringing.

"Where did all of them come from?" Artemis whispered softly, hoping by lowering her voice she wouldn't evoke such a violent reaction.

He watched her, and his hand twitched, causing her to flinch.

But this reaction of hers seemed enough to satiate him.

"Hired help," he said simply. "Everyone has a price. There are warlords who buy entire *armies*. We started by hunting. To see *who* could be trusted. If they refused to fire an arrow, we had them... taken care of."

Forester was still glaring at the man who'd struck her. Mattheus didn't seem to care.

Artemis stammered, "Why do this? I know... I know what happened to your daughter. She overdosed on drugs that Bateman was shipping here inside arrowheads. I know that she was sleeping with him."

At this part, Mattheus' eyes narrowed. "He was taking advantage of her. And then he killed her. And these elite... these *monsters,*" he said, snarling, waving his gun at the figures kneeling behind him. "Did nothing! None of them did. They sheltered him inside these golden gates. When I told the police, I was laughed at. Money doesn't just buy weapons, it buys power. Politics. It buys justice or mercy."

Artemis could feel her heart thumping even louder in her chest. She wanted to slink away, to hide.

But she had to take a stand.

"You don't have to do this," she said. "You can end this now."

"No," Mattheus said. "I can't. I have to show these people that there's a consequence for their actions. They have to pay for what happened to my daughter."

He turned to the figures, still kneeling, and sneered. "And you two. You have no idea what's coming for you. I'm going to make you both suffer."

He hoisted his gun, pointing it directly at the other two figures who gasped.

"NO!" Artemis shouted, her voice echoing through the room.

Mattheus laughed, his finger twitching on the trigger of his gun.

Words didn't work. It was the hardest lesson for Artemis. Sometimes words failed. Mercy failed.

But Forester wasn't encumbered by silly things like compassion or mercy.

Forester was a man of action. Justice, in a way, vengeance in another.

As Mattheus began to squeeze the trigger, Artemis realized why Cameron had been trying to reach her.

Not because he thought he could dodge bullets, but because he had been trying to get the guns to face him.

Away from her. Keeping her safe.

Now that the guns all pointed directly at him, he moved *fast*. His arm flung out with practiced precision.

He was a cage-fighter first. FBI second.

And standing this close, in the tight room, the nearest gunmen had made a fatal mistake.

Forester moved in a blur, twisting the arm of one man—there was a loud *snap* then a cry of pain. The second gunmen fired but missed, as Forester had shoved his hand to the side.

The bullet struck the leg of the third shooter in the doorway.

"Gun!" Forester yelled towards Artemis.

It was all he had time for.

Artemis lunged for the gun that the guy in the door had dropped. She snatched it off the ground even as his bloodied fingers tried to grab at her.

She avoided his grasp.

Mattheus was whirling around, his own gun raised.

"Forester!" she called.

And she flung the gun.

It all seemed to happen in slow motion. The gun she'd picked up from the man who'd been shot, arched through the air. Once, twice, in a blurring windmill of metal.

Forester reached out.

Mattheus turned and squeezed the trigger, his jacket shifting, revealing a radio transmitter on his belt. Likely the same one he'd used to speak to them back at the burnt mansion.

Forester caught the gun, dragging one of the other golden-masked thugs in front of him as he did.

The makeshift shield of meat was struck by Mattheus' first bullet.

And then Forester caught the gun, steadied, and fired twice.

Tap. Tap.

Two shots between Mattheus' eyes.

He toppled over. Dead.

But Forester was already moving, lunging towards the radio which had been at the madman's belt. He lifted the device, pressed a button, and said, his voice firm, "All units, stand down. Mattheus is dead. Cops are surrounding you. This is the FBI. Put your weapons down. I repeat, put your weapons down!"

His voice blared from the shoulder mics of the three golden-masked goons who were all groaning, clutching their wounds, and lying in pools of red on the ground.

The kneeling victims were sobbing now, hugging each other.

The older man spat towards Mattheus' corpse.

Artemis stared.

She felt sadness at how it had ended.

But relief that it had.

Her knees wobbled with exhaustion, and she leaned against a wall.

Chapter 30

Two shots. She hit the mark.

She turned, two more shots. Another hit. A flash of an image. The dead eyes of a madman staring at her. She shook the image from her head, aimed at the final cardboard cutout, and fired again.

A whistle blew.

"Well done!" called the FBI instructor.

A man wearing a black hat was watching her from a wooden platform, nodding as she lowered her weapon. He looked impressed.

Artemis was breathing heavily. Two weeks had now passed since the horrible events on the coast. And yet the dread she'd felt leading up to today, after the first rescheduling of her field test, was tantamount to what she'd experienced with a gun pressed to her neck.

She glanced at the small watch on her wrist.

She'd done it.

Two minutes under the limit. She let out a slow, relieved breath. And allowed herself a small smile.

And suddenly, she was tackled from behind.

"Wooot!" hollered a loud voice. "You did it! Way to go! You did it! Holy shit! I didn't think you had it in you!"

She grimaced, stumbling under his weight, but Cameron had caught her before she fell, wrapping his arms around her and holding her tight.

He was beaming from ear to ear as he stared at her.

She smiled up at his handsome face, still breathing heavily from the obstacle course and the shooting drill.

She shot another glance towards the FBI trainer standing on the platform. He was marking something on a plastic clipboard.

"I passed," she said.

Cameron nodded. "You sure did."

He kissed her forehead and hugged her tightly. She didn't pull away. Something had changed between them. She liked his touch. Liked standing close.

"We did it," she said.

She smiled and closed her eyes. She felt content. He wrapped his arms around her, still chortling softly.

And then she heard a soft *beep*.

She hesitated.

Another beep.

She glanced past Cameron's arm, still leaning against him, towards the bench where she'd left her phone and keys.

Her phone was chirping.

A notification she'd set up.

News about the shooting at the billionaire's community. She sighed as her phone screen lit up, illuminating the wooden varnish on the bench.

She shook her head, grimacing as she did. She then looked away.

Seven people had been killed before they'd reached the gated mansions. Mattheus had rigged explosions on two other houses, but the bomb squads had arrived in time.

With their leader dead, the hired men had taken no time in turning on each other.

She shivered.

The notifications were likely from various news sources, updating her on the trials.

She'd felt a grim attraction to the case's aftermath. They'd saved lives.

And taken them.

Forester didn't have any sense of the emotional storm she was enduring. Part of her wondered if he was more free than any of them. His inability to feel most emotions seemed like a gift at times... Though not always.

He wouldn't have wanted to give up his feelings for her. She didn't have to ask to know this.

But now, he was prattling happily, still wrapping his arms around her, while also trying to cop a feel. She pushed his hand away, and he smirked, like a child with their fingers caught in the cookie jar. "Sorry, my bad. Ask first. I remember."

She shook her head then stepped on his foot.

He yelped but then leaned in just as quickly, kissing her again.

The FBI instructor was glancing over now, watching curiously.

She felt her cheeks warm and pulled away. Now, she realized she was more amused than sad. Trust Forester to redirect her emotions. She also felt... aroused. Standing this close... Were they boyfriend and girlfriend? Less? More?

Hard to say.

"You look hot in those pants," Forester whispered in her ear.

"Yeah? You look hot without yours."

He stared at her and blinked. Then his smile widened. "Wanna go see if that theory holds?" he said, tugging her and trying to lead her to the nearest bathroom.

She smiled now. The fears, the worries, the pain she'd been experiencing were now fading away like mist under a sunset.

Her phone was still chirping though.

She slapped his ass as she passed, extricating herself and muttering, "One sec. Gotta check that."

The instructor was still watching them but looked away quickly after receiving a glare from Cameron. The sociopath shouted, "Take a picture, it'll last longer. Perv."

The instructor rolled his eyes. "You wish, Forester."

"Horny bastard," Forester shouted back.

The instructor raised a middle-finger. Forester returned the gesture.

Artemis just rolled her eyes and reached for her phone, feeling a slow elation fading once more as dread returned. What new horrible news would arrive from the case?

But as she thought this, and lifted the phone, she paused.

It wasn't a news bulletin.

It was a notification from her bank.

She stared at the account.

And then read the amount.

A deposit in her account.

One hundred million dollars.

The reward money for finding Kayla. This time, the small message in the wire transfer notes read *KB. Thanks for everything. Found Dad's note. I owe you.*

KB. Kayla Bateman. She'd followed through on her father's promise.

Kayla was alive.

Kayla had been taken care of by the paramedics, had survived. A flash of memory—charging through a burning building, snapping cuffs from a pipe.

And then the rescue.

Artemis found that it was difficult to breathe as she stared at her phone, and this had nothing to do with smoke inhalation.

She read the zeros again. Just to make sure.

And then she dropped her phone, her hand numb. She couldn't move. Not at first.

Forester was looking over now. "You okay?" he called.

She looked at him, eyes as wide as saucers.

And then, as if it had been pent up for weeks, months even, she began t
o *laugh* hysterically.

EPILOGUE

HE'D KILLED WOMEN BEFORE, and he'd enjoyed it.

But this time, he was determined to kill a man.

A very specific man.

The wounded soldier leaned back, his arms crossed, inhaling the sea breeze as the boat carried him across the waters, cutting towards the distant shores. He stared at the city skyline, watching, waiting.

His fingers tapped against his arm. His good arm.

The other was hollow. A prosthetic.

A small man nudged him, clearing his throat, but holding up a phone. "Here it is, sir. I confirmed it. It *is* him."

The wounded soldier nodded, staring at the picture. "Cameron Forester," he read slowly, and his words came painfully from a rasping throat. He scowled. Cameron was older now.

"Why isn't he dead?" the soldier said.

The small man with the black toupee shook his head. "I don't know," he whispered. "He should've been. When that boat blew up, he was on it."

"He thought he was killing me."

"Yes. Yes... for revenge."

The wounded soldier smiled, still staring at the screen. Ever since he'd killed Cameron Forester's wife, the ex-fighter had been on his trail. He'd shaken the bastard on an island... Set up another numbskull for the deed.

Cameron had killed the man, and then his boat had exploded.

But now, here he was. Alive and well and making news for saving lives during a shooting.

"He never could save lives," said the wounded soldier. And then he paused, frowning. "Who's this next to him? This woman?"

"Excuse me?"

"This woman?" he snapped, his hand tightening on the rail of the yacht. "Who is she? The mismatched eyes..."

He stared at the image, stunned. Perhaps he wasn't the only person who'd faked his death.

Cameron Forester's wife was *alive*?

Not possible.

But there she was, standing next to him. But no... no, her name was wrong. She was pretty, pale, but shorter than...

Yes. Not the same woman.

He let out a little breath, feeling a slow sense of relief.

"Maybe... maybe," his butler said quietly, "the *real* punishment wouldn't be to hurt Cameron. At least not at first."

"What are you saying?"

"Well?" A spindly finger tapped the page, pointing at the woman captioned as Artemis Blythe.

The yacht picked up pace now, moving through the waves, cutting towards the ports of Seattle. Towards Cameron Forester.

He had once promised the man he'd make him suffer. And the wounded soldier always kept his promises.

But his butler was right.

Forester's death wouldn't bring maximum suffering. But his new-found love interest?

This woman who looked remarkably similar to the man's deceased wife?

Now that was a fun thought.

He allowed his lips to curl into a smile, and then the plan began to change. "More articles. I need to read about them. Everything you can find."

"Of course. On it, sir.

It would take timing, preparation, wisdom... promises.

But Cameron Forester would suffer.

And now he knew exactly how to make that happen.

WHAT'S NEXT FOR ARTEMIS?

SHE QUIETLY SCREAMS

Victims are dying in public performance art, blackmailed into a suicidal spectacle...

Artemis' family is back together, and Helen thinks she knows who's committing the crimes. Artemis isn't sure she can trust her sister yet, but with no leads, and even less time, her back is against the wall, so she teams up with her sister to track a psycho.

Then, everything changes, when Jamie Kramer, Artemis' childhood sweetheart, is taken. The killer only targets people with deep secrets... And Artemis only knows of one secret that Jamie Kramer keeps on her behalf, which was the reason they broke up. During the performance art, the killer forces his victims to confess their deepest secrets to spectators, and now, not only does Artemis risk losing her ex, but her family's freedom is also on the line.

Will she be able to rescue Jamie in time? Or will another loved-one be stripped away by a deranged killer known only as the Director.

ALSO BY GEORGIA WAGNER

THE RIVERS SECRET

A cold knife, a brutal laugh.

Then the odds-defying escape.

Once a hypnotist with her own TV show, now, Sophie Quinn works as a full-time consultant for the FBI. Everything changed six years ago. She can still remember that horrible night. Slated to be the River

Killer's tenth victim, she managed to slip her bindings and barely escape where so many others failed. Her sister wasn't so lucky.

And now the killer is back.

Two PHDs later, she's now a rising star at the FBI. Her photographic memory helps solve crimes, but also helps her to never forget. She saw the River Killer's tattoo. She knows what he sounds like. And now, ten years later, he's active again.

Sophie Quinn heads back home to the swamps of Louisiana, along the Mississippi River, intent on evening the score and finding the man who killed her sister. It's been six years since she's been home, though. Broken relationships and shattered dreams exist among the bayous, the rivers, the waterways and swamps of Louisiana; can Sophie find her way home again? Or will she be the River Killer's next victim to float downstream?

ALSO BY GEORGIA WAGNER

GIRL UNDER THE ICE

Once a rising star in the FBI, with the best case closure rate of any investigator, Ella Porter is now exiled to a small gold mining town bordering the wilderness of Alaska. The reason for her new assignment? She allowed a prolific serial killer to escape custody.

But what no one knows is that she did it on purpose.

The day she shows up in Nome, bags still unpacked, the wife of the richest gold miner in town goes missing. This is the second woman to vanish in as many days. And it's up to Ella to find out what happened.

Assigning Ella to Nome is no accident, either. Though she swore she'd never return, Ella grew up in the small, gold mining town, treated like royalty as a child due to her own family's wealth. But like all gold tycoons, the Porter family secrets are as dark as Ella's own.

WANT TO KNOW MORE?

GREENFIELD PRESS IS THE brainchild of bestselling author Steve Higgs. He specializes in writing fast paced adventurous mystery and urban fantasy with a humorous lilt. Having made his money publishing his own work, Steve went looking for a few 'special' authors whose work he believed in.

Georgia Wagner was the first of those, but to find out more and to be the first to hear about new releases and what is coming next, you can join the Facebook group by copying the following link into your browser - www.facebook.com/GreenfieldPress.

ABOUT THE AUTHOR

GEORGIA WAGNER WORKED AS a ghost writer for many, many years before finally taking the plunge into self-publishing. Location and character are two big factors for Georgia, and getting those right allows the story to flow seamlessly onto the page. And flow it does, because Georgia is so prolific a new term is required to describe the rate at which nerve-tingling stories find their way into print.

When not found attached to a laptop, Georgia likes spending time in local arboretums, among the trees and ponds. An avid cultivator of orchids, begonias, and all things floral, Georgia also has a strong penchant for art, paintings, and sculptures. A many-decades long passion for mystery novels and years of chess tournament experience makes Georgia the perfect person to pen the Artemis Blythe series.

Printed in June 2023
by Rotomail Italia S.p.A., Vignate (MI) - Italy